SINFUL EMPIRE

BOOK THREE OF THE MOUNT TRILOGY

MEGHAN

USA TODAY BESTSELLING AUTHOR

MARCH

Copyright © 2017 by Meghan March LLC

ISBN: 978-1-943796-07-6

Editor: Pam Berehulke
Bulletproof Editing
www.bulletproofediting.com

Cover design: @ Letitia Hassar
RBA Designs
www.RBADesigns.com

Cover photo: @ Sara Eirew
www.saraeirew.com

Interior Formatting: Champagne Book Design

No part of this book may be reproduced or transmitted in any form or by any means, electronic or mechanical, including photocopying, recording, or by any information storage and retrieval system without the written permission of the author, except for the use of brief quotations in a review.

This book is a work of fiction. Names, characters, places, and incidents are either products of the author's imagination or are used fictitiously. Any resemblance to actual persons, living or dead, events, or locales is entirely coincidental. The author acknowledges the trademarked status and trademark owners of various products referenced in this work of fiction, which have been used without permission. The publication/use of these trademarks is not authorized, associated with, or sponsored by the trademark owners.

Visit my website at www.meghanmarch.com.

SINFUL EMPIRE

ABOUT THIS BOOK

What's mine, I keep, and that includes Keira Kilgore.

It's no longer enough to have her in my debt. No longer enough to own her body.

I want something more.

She can try to resist, but I'll never give her up.

Nothing will keep us apart.

Not her. Not my enemies. No one.

Her debt will only be paid one way—with her heart.

Sinful Empire is the third and final book in the Mount Trilogy.

ONE

Mount

Twenty-eight years earlier

"**Y**OU PIECE OF SHIT! GET BACK HERE! I'LL HAVE your ass in jail for this."

I plowed through the crowd, slamming into tourists and spinning around to lose the man charging after me. It was a total waste, because I didn't even get to use the distraction to lift more of their fat wallets or nice watches.

All because I'd wanted a goddamned Snickers bar to shut up my growling stomach for a couple hours, and didn't feel like parting with my hard-earned cash for it. Being a street kid in New Orleans wasn't for no weak-ass punks. The dark side of this town would chew you up and spit you out faster than you could spell *body bag*.

Don't make friends; make allies. But don't dare trust them further than you can see them.

"I see you, kid! Cops are coming! This time, you're done!"

Ernie, a douchebag convenience-store owner with the easiest candy to lift in the Quarter, was determined to get me sent up the river for good. But he had to catch me first.

Three years on the streets, and no one knew them better than me.

I slipped through the crowd, bolted down an alley, and squeezed between two bent rails in a wrought-iron fence. Ernie's fat ass would never be able to fit. I sprinted down a brick walkway and ran into a metal gate. *Locked.* Not a fucking problem for me.

I climbed it like a monkey and landed on my feet on the complete opposite side of the block. That asshole would never find me. I shoved my hands in my pockets and yanked out the wallets I'd picked before I hit Ernie's. I had to ditch them in case I got pinched.

I scanned the street, up and down, before I turned my back and flipped one open. I yanked out the two twenties inside. *Not bad.* I'd eat for a few weeks on that. I glanced at the ID it contained for a second before I tossed the wallet down the sewer drain.

Rocky Mount. Sounded like an asshole. Who would name their kid that?

As soon as the thought hit, I shut it down. At least they bothered to give their kid a name.

I flipped the second wallet open and found a crisp hundred. *Nice.* I'd be set for at least a couple months if I were careful, or if I wanted to risk it, I might be able to double my money.

I glanced at the second ID. *Lachlan Thorpe.* Better than Rocky Mount. A little, anyway.

I tossed the second wallet down the drain and

unwrapped the Snickers, then shoved the entire thing in my mouth to get rid of the rest of the evidence, chewing hard even as it stuck to my teeth. My stomach gnawed at my spine like it was eager for what was coming. I tried not to go more than a day or two without eating, but sometimes I didn't have a choice.

"I see you, punk!"

I swiveled my head in the direction of Ernie's voice.

Shit.

His bulk came hauling around the corner, two cops behind him, and I bolted in the opposite direction.

I was faster. Smarter. At least, that was what I told myself as I beat feet down the cracked pavement.

"Stop, kid!"

Footsteps pounded behind me, and I looked back as I hit the intersection instead of keeping my eyes forward.

Rookie mistake.

A black Mercedes blew through the stop sign and clipped me.

Shit, that hurts.

My body tensed at the impact but I tucked and rolled right up the hood. My elbows smashed into the windshield as the car slammed to a halt, throwing me forward again. Something jabbed into my side before I flipped off the metal and ate concrete.

Goddammit, that fucking hurts. I held in a groan as I planted my palms on the pavement and pushed off the ground.

Ernie and the cops, all yelling like idiots, closed in.

Unsteady, I shoved to my feet. I had to get out of here or I'd be done.

My ankle burned and gave out as I put weight on it, making me fall forward again, and I gripped the car to try to hold myself up. My ribs screamed in stabbing pain, but I clenched my teeth. Wasn't the first time I'd broken them, so I knew from experience how much this was gonna suck. I just had to get away. Find a place to pass out before the pain took me down right here. Because if I went down, I was really fucked.

The car doors opened—the driver's and one in the back—as I clung to the bent hood ornament to stay standing instead of hitting my knees again.

Damn rich people in their nice-ass cars with these fancy hood ornaments.

"Don't you fucking move, kid! You're going to jail this—"

Ernie's words cut off, and black spots dotted my vision as I tried to focus. Both the store owner and the two cops behind him stood stock-still in the middle of the street.

"Mr. Morello, so sorry, sir. We'll take this piece of trash out of your way." That came from one of the cops.

"Care to explain what's going on here, gentlemen?" The voice was deep and had a faint Italian accent.

Morello. Morello. My brain wasn't working like it should, but the name was right there. I should know it. Morello.

"Just a street kid shoplifting. Been trying to catch him for damn near two years now."

A deep laugh followed Ernie's explanation.

"So either he's smart as hell, or you're all fucking incompetent. Which is it?" The man's tone held no respect for Ernie or the cops, and it clicked in my head.

4

Holy shit. Morello was Johnny Morello, current acting head of the Morello crime family. They ran this town. Owned this town.

I was screwed, any way I looked at it. I fucked up Morello's car, and his goon would probably put a bullet in my head for it while the cops watched, their dicks in their hands, because they couldn't touch him. No one could. And if the goon didn't kill me, he'd leave me for the cops and Ernie to deal with, and there was no doubt in my mind I was going down. They were trying kids as adults these days for everything they could. No doubt, Ernie would make it his mission to land me in prison for life.

From my bent-over position hanging on to the car to stay upright, I watched as two shiny black leather shoes stepped into my line of sight. I swallowed the urge to puke my guts all over the Mercedes and the shoes, and instead forced myself to stand straight despite the burning and stabbing pain in my ribs as I breathed.

"What's your name, kid?" Morello's question was quiet but carried the unmistakable weight of authority. From everything I'd heard, he was a man you didn't fuck with and live.

I met his gaze, determined to show no fear, which was more than I could probably say for Ernie and the cops. *Bet they're pissing themselves right now.*

I hadn't had a name in the two years I'd been living on these streets. I'd left Michael Arch behind the Dumpster I used for cover while I watched the social worker pick up Hope and Destiny from the church shelter. I was born nameless, so I lived nameless. But I couldn't tell that to Johnny Morello. And I sure as shit wouldn't give him the name Michael Arch. Far as I knew, he was still wanted for murder.

"I don't repeat myself, kid."

Someone nudged me from behind and I straightened, my ribs crying in pain I'd never show.

Morello's black eyes drilled into me as my brain scrambled for something to tell him. I remembered the IDs I just tossed down the gutter, and made something up.

"Name's Lachlan Mount, sir. I apologize for the damage I caused. It wasn't intentional. I meant no disrespect."

Morello studied me, no doubt taking in my roughed-up appearance, hard eyes, and sharp features. "Lachlan Mount. Strong name for a smart kid. Is that what you are, Mount?"

"Yes, sir."

"You been dodging the cops for two years?" His eyes narrowed on me like he was waiting for me to lie. But Morello didn't realize I had nothing to lose anymore.

"Yes, sir."

His dark eyebrows raised ever so slightly. "Today didn't work out how you planned, then."

"No, sir. Not at all." I gritted my teeth as the pain intensified the longer I stood up straight.

"You fucked my car up, Mount. You owe me for that."

I nodded and reached into my pocket to pull out the cash I'd just lifted. "My apologies, sir." I handed it out toward him. "This is everything I got."

He looked down at the bills in my hand and laughed, a deep booming noise that seemed to echo off the tall brick buildings hemming us in and blocking my escape.

"You know how much this car costs, kid? Because what

you got there won't even fix the hood ornament."

"It's all I got, sir."

I waited for the press of a barrel to my head from behind, because I'd heard these Mafia types preferred execution-style, but it didn't come.

Morello tilted his head to the side, studying me. "How long did it take you to steal that money?"

"A few minutes. Grabbed 'em on my way to that fat fuck's store."

"Hey—" Ernie yelled, ready to defend himself, but Morello raised a hand and he instantly went silent.

Morello rubbed a hand across his dark mustache that was already going silver and studied me some more. "How old are you, Mount?"

The more he said the name I'd just picked, the more I liked it. It felt right. Like I was born to it.

I straightened my shoulders, despite the blinding pain. I had pride, and that was stronger. "Fifteen, almost sixteen." I made up the last part because I didn't have a clue when my birthday actually was.

Morello dropped his hand from his mustache and drilled me with a stare. "You got three choices today, Mount, because I'm feeling generous."

I kept quiet, waiting to hear what judgment he was gonna deliver.

"One, I hand you over to the cops and they try you as an adult, toss your ass in prison. I doubt you make it a day before you're someone's favorite bitch."

I forced myself not to react, even though his statement made me want to hurl my guts up, because I knew he was right.

"Two, Frankie will shoot you right here for fucking up my favorite car, and we'll leave your body in the gutter, which is probably where you figured you'd die."

He wasn't wrong about that, but I didn't say shit to reply.

"Or three, you get in the backseat, we take you to the doc to get patched up, and you work your debt off to me until you've paid for every penny of repairs to my car. If you don't fuck that up, we'll see how you fit in, and maybe you'll have yourself a real job instead of picking tourist pockets."

One of the cops finally found the balls to speak. "Mr. Morello, sir, we can take him from here. There's no need for you to bother yourself with—"

Morello's attention snapped toward him, cutting off his words. "If I wanted your opinion, pig, I'd ask for it. Now, shut the fuck up."

His gaze cut back to mine as I heard the slide of a gun. I assumed it was Frankie, Morello's goon, getting ready to either carry out option two or kill a cop in broad daylight.

My insides turned liquid, but I wouldn't show fear. I made the only decision I could.

"Three, sir. I choose option three."

Morello nodded. "That's what I figured, because you're not a fucking moron like those assholes." He jerked his head at the cops before glancing over my shoulder. "Put him in the car. Call Doc. Have him meet us."

As soon as the man's hands landed on me, I spun around, grinding my teeth to keep from screaming out in pain. "I can help myself into the car."

A glimmer of amusement flitted through Frankie's eyes. "Get in the front seat, kid."

I hobbled toward the door and opened it, practically collapsing inside before slamming it shut. Thankfully, no one could hear my hiss of pain because Morello and Frankie were still outside, facing Ernie and the cops. Their voices came loud and clear through the open back door.

"Sir, with all due respect—"

"You've never heard the name Lachlan Mount. You will never repeat it. You've never seen him before. You will forget he exists. He's part of my organization now, and if you so much as think about going after him, I'll watch while my people skin you alive and laugh when you squeal like the pigs you are. Then I'll put bullets in the heads of everyone you love. How's that sound?"

All three men, including the two in uniform, bobbed their heads like idiots and sputtered out replies.

"Understood, sir."

"Never heard of him before."

"Don't know who you're talking about, Mr. Morello. We're just heading back to the station."

Their fear of Morello rolled off them like stink. Or maybe one of them shit themselves. From the way the cops' legs were quivering, I'd believe it. And then there was the wet spot spreading down Ernie's pants.

He really did piss himself. *No fucking way.*

Then again, I wasn't surprised. Morello's posture was rigid. His orders absolute. I had no doubt in my mind he'd kill them all right here and follow through on everything he said.

I'd never seen that kind of power in action before. Never seen that kind of fear on any cop's face. I soaked it up.

What would it be like to command that kind of respect?

Morello climbed into the backseat of the Mercedes, and Frankie closed the door.

"Don't make me regret this, Mount, because I will fucking bury you alive if you betray me or mine."

"Understood, sir. You won't regret it."

"Good."

Frankie climbed in and fired up the busted car that saved my life. Somewhere along the bumpy ride to wherever the hell we were going, I silently passed out from the pain.

TWO

Keira

Present day

PAIN SLICES THROUGH ME AS I REGAIN CONSCIOUSNESS. The car door flies open, and gravity sends me tilting to the side. Strong arms stop my fall.

"I got you. Open your eyes, hellion. Open your fucking eyes for me. Goddammit, I'm not going to lose you now."

That voice. Deep. Dark. Rough. It was the voice of the devil, but not anymore. Now it's the voice of the man I was furious I wasn't going to be allowed to keep after we returned to New Orleans.

My eyelids flicker open, and I feel like there's a dent where my skull smacked the window as we hurtled around the corner and plowed through a lamppost. A headache pounds relentlessly in my temple. When I meet the familiar dark gaze, his dread morphs into relief. The burning heat in those eyes used to send tremors of fear shuddering through me, but now it gives me strength.

"Thank fucking Christ." His forehead touches mine lightly, and I breathe in his woodsy citrus scent.

"You think you're going to get rid of me that easily?" My words come out weak and slurred, with none of the confidence I intended. I try to sit up, but pain stabs into my right side. "Dammit, that hurts. What happened?"

"Doesn't matter. You're gonna be fine. I swear to you on my life that *you will be fine.*"

The way he says it, with absolute conviction underlying every word, I believe him.

I drop my gaze from his and take in the blood covering my shirt and the shards of glass everywhere. "Oh shit."

His big hand grips my chin and brings my attention back up to his eyes, but not before I see the red staining his clothes as well.

"Oh God. We need help."

"We're going to be fine. Understand me? You need to hold it together. Can you do that?"

I nod as my skull threatens to crack from the thumping. Bile rises in my throat.

"Block out the pain, Keira. You can do it."

I take a shallow breath and shudder. "I can do it," I say, no clue if I'm lying or not.

"Good girl." He rips off his suit jacket and presses it against my side. "Hold this tight, like your fucking life depends on it. You got me?"

When Lachlan Mount says to do something like your life depends on it, it actually might. I remember the dread I saw in his eyes only moments before.

"Am I dying?" Instead of sadness, anger rushes in. *I'm*

not ready. I'm not done with this world. I'm not done with this man.

"You are not fucking dying. I won't allow it." His words are backed by steely determination and raw tenacity.

"Okay." I press the jacket tighter against the source of the pain in my right side as he slides an arm around my back.

"We're getting the fuck out of here. My people are on their way. Hold tight."

I give him another nod, stars bursting in my vision with every movement as Lachlan lifts me out of the car, staying low and rounding the rear of it to pause between the crumpled front end and the building it crashed into. He stumbles with a grunt, and the sound of his suffering spears into me worse than my own.

"Stop. You're hurt. Don't—"

"Not until you're safe. Not taking any fucking chances with you. Where the hell are they?" His head swivels from side to side as my vision threatens to go dark again.

What's wrong with my head?

I force the fuzziness down because there's no way I'm passing out again. I'm stronger than that.

I squeeze his hand in an effort to get his attention. "I'm not losing you either. Do you understand me? Stop being such a stubborn bastard."

His gaze drops to me, and any evidence of the pain he felt a moment ago seems to vanish as one corner of his mouth quirks up. "Deal."

Tires screech and I turn my head, wincing as agony shoots through my temples. Only I can't see anything because Lachlan angles us away from the street, gripping me tighter and turning his back to the oncoming car. *Using himself as a human shield.*

"Don't you dare—"

"Shut up, Keira. When it comes to you, I'll do whatever I have to." His big hand cups the back of my head and presses it against his chest.

Another car screeches to a halt, and the sound of doors opening penetrates my pounding head. Footsteps thump against the pavement as Lachlan turns his head.

"Thank fuck," he whispers, his body relaxing as he swivels around and I catch sight of Scar.

Another face that used to inspire fear now only brings relief. Scar bolts toward us, as silent as always, but fierce rage is stamped on his every feature.

Lachlan clasps me tighter against his chest. "Take her. Lock her down. Your life for hers. Understand me?"

The silent man nods, and Lachlan loosens his grip on me. "Don't you fucking die on me, Keira. I swear I'll rip down those pearly gates and come for you myself."

Scar's arms form a cradle around me, a hold I know all too well, but my fingers won't release their grip on Lachlan's collar. The fabric stretches as Scar steps away, tearing my grip free.

"I'm not leaving you!" I struggle in Scar's arms, even though every moment makes my stomach roil and my body cry out for me to stop. "Put me down. I'm staying with him."

Scar grunts in my ear, and my gaze fixes on the shirt Lachlan's wearing. The left side is completely soaked through with red. At first, I think it's mine, but the torn fabric and the steadily pumping flow tell me I'm wrong.

"Leave me! Save him! He needs you more." Tears flow down my face as Scar holds me tighter, not letting my pathetic struggles deter him from taking me farther and farther away from Lachlan.

Two other men rush toward us, but I don't know them.

"Kill them!" I scream, not recognizing my own voice. "Don't you fucking touch him, you bastards!"

Lachlan staggers and the men catch him, one on either side.

"Get her safe—" His voice cuts off as his body goes slack in the arms of the two strangers.

"No!" I scream, but Scar continues toward the car, not acknowledging what just happened. "Stop! You have to go back for him!"

I fight his grip on me, clawing at his shoulders, uncaring about the anguish tearing through my body. Horror drowns out the pain as they drag Lachlan's limp body toward a car I don't recognize, and Scar heads for the familiar one.

"Let me go!" I shout, but my voice breaks as he lowers me into the backseat and slams the door in the face of my protests.

I grope at the handle, desperate to stop the men from hauling Lachlan away, but Scar is already in the front seat. The doors lock before he slams the car in drive and speeds down a street in the French Quarter.

Weeks ago, I would have rejoiced at being driven in a speeding car in the opposite direction of Lachlan Mount, but that was before. What he said in the hangar was right. *Everything has changed.*

Tears pour down my face in rivers as I turn to look out

the tinted back window. In the rapidly increasing distance, two men load Lachlan's lifeless body into the backseat of the other sedan.

My voice goes hoarse as I scream at Scar to take me back, but we turn a corner and I lose sight of him.

"No!"

THREE

Keira

I DON'T REMEMBER PASSING OUT, BUT WHEN I WAKE UP IN a room dominated by white walls, an industrial gray floor, and the scent of antiseptic, I know I must have lost consciousness.

I jerk up in the hospital bed, my head swiveling from side to side. *Bad move.* The thumping gets worse, and so does my fuzzy vision.

But through the haze, I make out another bed lying empty a half-dozen feet away from mine.

Where is he? Thoughts of Lachlan being dragged away by strangers play like a nightmare through my brain. I have to find him.

Leads are attached to my chest, and I rip them off. The steady beeping of the equipment shrieks with an alarm.

I'm still attached to an IV, but I tear off the tape and prepare to yank it out. The door flies open, and a woman I've never seen before enters.

"Stop. You rip that out and we'll just have to put another

17

in. He insisted we not take any chances with you. Overkill all the way, in my opinion, but I'm not the boss."

"Where is he?" My fingers grip the tubing like I'm a psych patient with a knife to my wrist. "Tell me, or I'll have this out before you can take another step."

Her head jerks back at the vehemence of my threat. "Docs are with him now, patching him up. No need to tear yourself apart and get him pissed at me because of it."

My hand goes limp.

"Patching him up? How bad is it?" I remember the tear in his shirt and the blood pumping from the hole in his side. "What happened? Where am I?"

My memories are even more shattered than the night I got drunk in Dublin. *The night I danced with Lachlan in a pub.*

She responds to my questions out of order. "You're in the clinic in the compound. We're self-sufficient here. Mount was shot, a through-and-through. You've got a hell of a concussion on top of superficial cuts, bruising, and a decent-sized laceration on your right side. You were lucky it wasn't deeper. Didn't need sutures, just Dermabond. We cleaned you up and ran a bunch of tests. You're going to be just fine."

I look down at the blue hospital scrubs I'm wearing as though I can see through them. "Cuts and bruises and a concussion? Shouldn't that hurt more?"

The woman, who I now assume is either a doctor or a nurse, laughs. "Honey, you're doped up on enough pain-killers that you should be feeling like a champ. Just . . . don't rip the IV out. It's messy. We've cleaned up plenty of blood already today."

Enough about me.

"How long until he's back? How bad was the gunshot? He's going to be okay, right? He said he'd be okay. He promised."

She studies me like I'm some kind of wild creature, and right now, that's exactly what I feel like.

"He lost a hell of a lot more blood than you did. Didn't even bother to try and stop the bleeding, and he knows better than that."

My foggy memory recalls him giving me his jacket to stop my bleeding. *Possibly at the expense of his own life.*

"He's not going to die." It's not a question. It can't be, because I'll lose it.

But the nurse or doctor, or whoever the hell she is, agrees. "No. You're right. He's not going to die. He's too damn stubborn. Even the devil would send him right back."

A tiny sliver of relief works its way into the panic crushing my chest.

"You're sure?"

She gives me a nod. "He's got a couple overqualified docs working on him. Only the best for Mount. But the stubborn ass wouldn't let them touch him until they were done treating you."

"What?" My voice breaks.

"He pulled a gun on them and everything."

That sounds exactly like the man I know and love.

Wait.

Love?

The word crashes through my brain like the bullet that apparently shattered the windshield of the car.

Is that even . . . possible?

I slump back on the bed, my strength sapped, and she comes closer.

"Are you okay, Ms. Kilgore?"

Am I okay?

I don't know how to answer. Right now, I'm grappling with the most shocking—but obvious—realization of my life.

I'm falling in love with Lachlan Mount.

Scratch that. Not falling. *I've fallen.*

"Ms. Kilgore? Is something wrong? Are you in pain?"

I shake my head. "It's not that. I'm . . . it's just . . ."

Her eyes turn sympathetic. "Delayed shock?"

"Maybe." The pillow cradles my head as I stare up at the ceiling and come to terms with the truth.

I've heard traumatic experiences can have a very crystalizing effect on your thoughts, but how could I have missed that this was building beneath the surface?

"Dance with me, Lachlan. Dance with me in Dublin."

His smile from that night flashes through my brain. Is that when it happened? Does it matter?

"Let me reattach these leads so we can keep an eye on you. I'm pretty sure he'd literally kill me if I let anything happen to you now."

She tapes my IV back down and then moves toward the machine, straightening out the tangled leads I ripped off before reattaching them to me, but I'm not paying attention to her at all.

Which is probably why I miss whatever else she adds to the mix pumping through my IV until she speaks.

"You need to rest," she says as she removes the bag that was hanging there.

"What did you do?"

"Just gave you a little something to help keep you comfortable."

My eyes grow heavy and I open my mouth to protest, but I'm no match for whatever drugs she sent pumping through me.

"He'll be here when you wake up."

FOUR

Mount

KEIRA'S SCREAMS ECHO IN MY BRAIN ON REPEAT AS I thrash against the sheets and drag myself from an uneasy sleep. *What the fuck did they give me?* I told them I didn't need shit. I needed to stay aware. On guard.

The same thoughts have been on repeat in my brain since that fucking bullet slammed through the windshield. *I can't lose her. Don't you fucking take her from me.*

"Where is she?" My voice sounds hoarse to my own ears when it finally cooperates, but there's no way to miss the desperation underlying my demand. "Is Keira okay?"

"I'm right here."

Keira's small hand closes over mine. The tension leaves my body at her touch, even as the scent of disinfectant fills my nose.

"I made them move you closer to me since they threatened to handcuff me to this bed to keep me in it when I tried to get to yours."

Her voice is husky and barely loud enough to hear

over the beeping of the machines, but her words wrap around me, settling me down even more. How I earned that kind of loyalty from her, I'll never understand. I'll never let her take it back, either.

I scan every inch of her body, from her messy red hair down to the blue scrubs she's wearing. No signs of blood anymore. She's in one piece, and her face isn't pinched with pain.

"Please fucking tell me you're okay." In my nightmare, she was screaming because she was dying, and I couldn't save her. Those screams were worse than the pain of any of the bullets I've had punch through my body. A million times worse than being hit by that Mercedes so fucking long ago. Worse than any stab wound or other injury I've endured or could imagine.

"I'm fine. You're gonna be fine. We're both going to be fucking fine, or I swear to God, I will hunt down whoever did this and kill them myself." Icy determination backs her every word.

My bloodthirsty hellion. My defiant queen.

I shouldn't smile about it, but when it comes to this woman, nothing is rational. She came from a bubble, a world that I've never inhabited. When I dragged her into the shadows and darkness, I gave no thought to the consequences of my actions beyond the satisfaction I would gain from her submission.

I'm a selfish man. I know myself well enough to accept it. I take, and take, and take.

That's what I intended to do with Keira Kilgore. Take her until I was sated. But tonight, the only thing I wanted to take was every single bit of her pain, regardless of whether it killed me.

I've never believed in selflessness. I thought it was a myth. But where Keira Kilgore is concerned, my beliefs have shifted.

Everything has shifted.

Life taught me not to get attached to a single fucking thing, because nothing in this world is permanent. Everything is temporary.

I no longer accept that when it comes to her. She's mine. She's staying mine. Even my black heart couldn't handle losing her. I will keep her safe with my very last breath, if necessary.

I've avoided weakness like other men avoid the devil . . . or me. But I didn't care about weakness in the moments when I thought I might lose her. That's when something else became clear—losing Keira Kilgore would mean losing my strength.

This fiery redhead, with sparks flaring in her green eyes, shifted the foundation of my whole world.

"I thought I lost you," she says, her gaze filling with anguish. "I never want to feel like that again."

"Never. The devil won't even take me."

"Promise me."

Nothing is permanent, my inner voice reminds me. But I'm Lachlan fucking Mount, and I make the rules and can change them anytime I want.

"I promise."

She squeezes my hand tighter. "Good."

"I should make you go. Send you somewhere safe, as far away from me as I can get you, but—"

"I dare you to try." Keira lifts her stubborn chin.

"If I were a better man, that's exactly what I would do."

Her expression turns mulish, her jaw clenching. "Then it's a good thing you're not."

The door opens, and one of the docs whose name I can't remember comes in. "Mr. Mount, how are you feeling?"

My first reaction should be to drop Keira's hand, to make sure he doesn't see how fucking gone I am for her, because it would be an admission of weakness. But that's not at all what I do.

Instead, I thread my fingers through hers, and we present a united front to him.

"Like I've been fucking shot and sewn up."

"I can have the nurse increase your pain meds. You won't feel anything then."

He backs away toward the door, and I stop him.

"No. You already gave me too much. I don't want anything else. I want to feel it. Every single fucking bit of it. I'm not letting you knock me out again."

"Lachlan—" Keira's voice is low, and her squeeze of my hand is tight. When I squeeze back, she goes silent.

"Make sure Ms. Kilgore has all the pain meds and everything else she needs, but leave my shit alone. Tell V to get in here when you leave."

The doctor nods and turns to retreat, his stare sweeping across our joined hands.

"Breathe a word of what happened tonight, and—"

"I wouldn't dare, sir. Hit the call button if either of you need anything at all. We're at your service for as long as you need."

As soon as he leaves the room, Keira jerks her hand

out of mine. I want to snatch it back, but she's too busy wagging a finger in my face.

"Don't you try to tough out the pain like a stubborn ass. Take the drugs."

I turn toward her, my body protesting against the movement, but I need to see her face so she understands exactly why I refused them.

"If I'm under, I can't protect you, and that's not an option. You're tied to me. Your safety—your life—is in my hands, and that's not something I'm willing to risk just to save myself a few hours of pain."

"A few hours?" She scoffs. "You were shot. It's not like it was a freaking paper cut."

"It wasn't the first time. Probably won't be the last."

Keira growls, and it's clear that any fear she used to have of me, even well-masked fear, is gone completely. "Don't you dare get shot again."

"I can't promise you that."

"Then lie to me. Give me something."

A rough laugh rumbles up from deep inside me. *One of a kind.* I knew it before, and she's proven it every day since.

Lies. They've always fallen so easily from my lips. Second nature. First choice. But in this instance, I can't do it.

"No more lies. Not between us. Not anymore."

Keira's head jerks back, shock flashing across her features. "Does that mean you're going to tell me all your secrets if I ask?"

I glance toward the ceiling. Of course she would go there. She wouldn't be the partner I never knew I wanted—never knew I needed—if she didn't.

I release a long breath, a large part of me not believing what I'm about to do. But like I realized earlier, *everything* has changed.

"What do you want to know?"

FIVE

Keira

NO. FREAKING. WAY.

He's not giving me carte blanche to ask him any question and be told the truth, is he? But the sincerity in his dark gaze can't be denied. Then again, neither can the fatigue lining his features.

Before, I would have jumped at the chance to give this man the third degree and get the answers to all the questions I've been storing up, but right now, I can't do it. Instead, I focus on him, and getting him well.

Because Lachlan's health and safety shot to the top of my priority list the moment I watched them drag him away from me in the street.

"You need to sleep. Rest. Because you have hell to rain down on this city so everyone knows that no one fucks with Lachlan Mount or his woman."

Again, shock flashes over his face, and he stares at me like he's never seen me before. Maybe he's right. Because I've never felt like this before.

"My woman?"

I narrow my eyes on him. "You're the one who wanted me to admit that I'm yours. Turns out, life-and-death experiences have a way of clarifying things pretty damn quickly."

His gaze shutters before he speaks. "It's the drugs talking. By the time you're out of that bed, you'll be railing against me again, demanding I let you go."

I purse my lips and cross my arms over my chest, hiding the wince of pain that breaks through the pain meds they've pumped into my body.

Is it the meds? I refuse to believe it. The possessiveness I felt, and the willingness to claw through glass to get to him as he was taken away from me, was no function of drugs. Adrenaline, maybe. But it was the absolute truth.

"I guess we'll see who's right about that. Because I already know exactly how this is going to play out."

"And how's that?" he asks, but the door opens before I can answer.

SIX

Mount

A S SOON AS V WALKS IN, I CAN READ EVERYTHING I need to know in the expression on his face. Shit is bad. *Really bad.*

I learned long ago that if he's not texting me, the only way to get answers is yes-and-no questions. And because my phone is nowhere to be found, yes-and-no questions are my only choice.

"Have they found the shooter?" I didn't have to give that order. J would already be searching as soon as the report came in about what happened.

V shakes his head.

"Did they take care of the cops?" Someone would have called in the accident, and I need the cops who might have made it to the scene before it was cleaned up to forget anything they saw. No one can know about what happened. It would upset the power balance if word got around that someone had the balls to try to take me out. Luckily, a solid chunk of the cops in this city answer to me rather than the other way around.

V nods.

"Was the car towed to the garage and the scene swept?"

Another nod.

"Bullet retrieved?"

He holds up a hand with two fingers about an inch apart. I know that means *not yet, but they're close.*

"Tear that car apart. The bullet's gotta be in there. I didn't see an exit hole. Find out where the fuck it came from and trace the shooter. We need to know who the hell was stupid enough to attempt this."

Another nod. V turns to leave, but I stop him.

"You did good. Her safety is always your first priority—no matter what. You always see to her first, just like you did."

Keira pipes up, interrupting the conversation. "Uh, no. I disagree with that."

I shoot a look at her. "You don't get a say in this. It's not something I'll ever compromise on."

"Not at the expense of your own safety. Don't make me bear that burden. The price is too steep."

V swings his gaze between us, no doubt shocked at the new subject of our argument.

"Who do your orders come from, V?" I snap, bringing his attention back to me. When he obediently points at me, I look at Keira. "Doesn't matter what you say, I overrule."

"I'm calling bullshit."

"Too damn bad."

V meets my gaze once more, and I speak my next words to him.

"Stand guard. No one gets in unless there's a medical

emergency, and then only approved staff. I'm told I need to rest so I can rain hell down on this city and whoever did this." I glance at Keira with a crooked smile.

V nods and heads for the door.

Once it closes behind him, fatigue weighs down my limbs, but I still reach out my hand to clasp Keira's, and she squeezes it.

This whole experience—her not fighting me, not trying to escape—is surreal. And so is me following her orders.

"I won't let you—"

I cut her off with a glance. "I thought you wanted me to rest so I can be ready to exact vengeance."

Her eyebrows wing up in the direction of her hairline. "You're actually going to listen to me?"

"On one condition."

"Name it," she says without hesitation.

"You rest too."

Her mouth screws up into a defiant expression, but for a completely different reason this time. "I'll keep watch. You rest."

"V is outside on guard. No one's getting through him. So, please, fucking rest. I need you whole and healthy. I have a lot of plans for you, woman."

Keira studies me for long moments before she finally responds. "And you will if I will?"

"Yes."

"Deal."

She reaches out her hand and I shake it, sealing the bargain.

Somehow, in the midst of chaos, our positions changed. No longer am I the one forcing her to bend to my wishes because she has no other options. Now, we're equals. Partners.

It's a new and different feeling, one that should scare the shit out of me, but it feels *nothing* like weakness. Actually, I've never felt stronger.

I drift off, my fingers still tangled with hers.

SEVEN

Keira

EVEN DRUGGED BY THE PAIN MEDS, I WAKE UP FIRST. I think I forced my body to allow me to regain consciousness because I needed to reassure myself that Lachlan was still breathing.

I couldn't care less about my injuries now. I'm much more concerned about him. The strain is visible on his face, even in sleep.

I swore I'd hate him until my dying breath. That I'd never give him what he wanted. That I'd build impenetrable walls around my heart, even if he messed with my head and forced my body to betray me.

Lachlan Mount destroyed those walls. When he turned his back, using himself as a shield, it became pretty damned clear where I stood with him, and that was before I knew he'd already been shot.

But if I'm completely honest, that's not when my walls started to crumble. No, that mortar began to break down the moment I realized he was taking me to Dublin, fulfilling a lifelong dream of mine, even though there was nothing in it for him.

I may not have had the chance to ask my questions yet, but I'm willing to bet everything I own on the fact that self-less actions are new for Lachlan Mount.

The door to the room opens again, and V steps inside. Another shift, because I'm no longer thinking of him as Scar. He's not the man who aids and abets my captivity, but someone who was also willing to lay down his life for mine.

"Is everything okay?" I whisper.

I know he won't answer me, and even though Magnolia said it's because Lachlan cut out his tongue, I'm one hundred percent certain that she's wrong. Loyalty like V shows to his boss isn't born of fear and intimidation. It's a product of respect.

V nods, but holds something out to me.

My purse. And in his other hand? My phone.

He lays both on the bed beside me, nodding down at the phone insistently.

I glance at the screen and see several missed calls from my father and text messages from Temperance.

Shit. It's one o'clock in the afternoon, and a day later than I realized.

I slept a lot longer than I thought.

It doesn't help that I've lost track of time, what with the time change from our flight, the drugs, and the lack of a clock in this room.

I unlock the screen and read the texts first.

TEMPERANCE: *Our phones are ringing off the hook. Your dad. The press. The tourism board. Distributors.*

> *Everyone wants to know about the award from the*
> *GWSC. I know it was a last-minute plan to go, but*
> *I gotta tell them something, boss. Help me out here.*
> TEMPERANCE: *Are you okay? Where are you?*
> TEMPERANCE: *Keira, please freaking answer me. Your*
> *dad said he's getting on a plane tomorrow morning*
> *and heading here.*

The time stamp on the last text message is an hour ago.

Shit. I don't want my dad *anywhere* near New Orleans right now. Not with the situation I've landed myself in. Lachlan swore to me he'd keep my family safe, and I believe him, but I still don't want them here.

Checking the bars of service, I find that I have none.

I glance back up at V. "I need to make calls. Text people. You've gotta help me. I have to stop my dad from coming."

V glances at Lachlan's sleeping form in the bed, and then back to me. His loyalties are clearly torn.

"I only need a few minutes. Please. This is important. Believe me when I tell you I wouldn't be asking to leave his side if it wasn't."

Something gets through to him, either in my words or my tone, and he nods before holding up a finger. Basically, the universal gesture for *hold on a second*. He leaves the room and returns moments later with the nurse who told me not to rip the IV from my hand.

"Do you need something? What's wrong?" The nurse looks from me to Lachlan.

"I need you to unhook me. I have to make some calls. It's incredibly important."

She narrows her eyes. "Did Mount approve this?"

"Do you want to be the one to explain to him why you won't follow a simple order? Because at this point, I promise you that he'll consider denying my request to be tantamount to denying his." My tone invites no argument, and each word is backed with confident authority.

My statement knocks her back on her heels, and she deliberates for less than a minute. "Give me a moment to unhook you, ma'am."

The respect in her voice is undeniable. Her movements are quick and efficient as she removes the leads from my chest and unhooks my IV.

"You don't need this anymore, but you better tell him you made me take it out, or I'll have hell to pay."

"Don't worry about it. I can handle him." I glance at V as he silently waits for me. "Go handpick someone to take your place outside the room. Someone you trust with his life." I jerk my head at Lachlan's sleeping form.

V nods at this command, once again holding up a finger before disappearing.

I'm on my feet, more unsteady than I want to admit, when he returns and leads me out of the room. I don't recognize the two men outside the door at first, but I know I've seen them before.

They're the ones who caught Lachlan when he fell.

"Leave him unattended for even a second, and I'll kill you both myself. Do you understand me?" I make the threat without hesitation, and the shock on both men's faces is nearly comical.

Somehow, I'm less surprised that I gave the order than how good it feels to give it. At this point, I'm willing to follow through on a lot of things I never expected to consider.

I sold my body to keep my family and friends safe. Now, I'd sell my soul to keep Lachlan from harm.

"Yes, ma'am. No one will get through us," one of the men replies.

I give them both a nod, and they return the gesture with deferential respect.

The shifts just keep coming.

I'm no longer a prisoner. I'm the consort to the king.

"Where the hell have you been? I've been trying to get in touch with you for freaking ever," Temperance says in lieu of a greeting.

My head aches as I hold the phone to my ear, but I push the pain away. "There was an unforeseen delay in my return from Dublin. I'm sorry I wasn't able to get in touch before now." I'm proud of how professional my bullshit excuse sounds, and the fact that my voice is steady.

"Unforeseen delay?" Her tone is skeptical, at best.

"Fill me in on what's happening first so we can triage, and then I have things I need to tell you. Things that you can't repeat to anyone. And I mean *anyone*."

My assistant goes quiet. "Keira, does this have to do with the chauffeur you suddenly acquired a couple weeks ago?"

It doesn't surprise me that she noticed V driving me, but I am surprised she hasn't brought it up until now.

"Yes, but first, business. Then I tell you the rest."

Temperance launches into the list of things that require my attention, all stemming from the announcement of the

Spirit of New Orleans taking home a prestigious award. An award that I now think might have saved me by taking the brunt of the bullet after it left Lachlan's body. It would make the most sense given the laceration they glued shut on my right side, which was where the glass bottle was sitting in my lap and is probably still in the shot-up car. None of which I'm going to tell Temperance.

"So, the press wants a statement and a release date for sale to the general public. The tourism board wants to know how quickly we can start tours because of the press interest. Your dad wants to know how the hell you found the money to go to the GWSC. Oh, and every distributor we have wants to know when they're going to be able to get their hands on it."

I take a slow, shallow breath, cognizant of my weakened state, and give myself two seconds to absorb all the information and center myself back in CEO mode.

"Write up a press release. Tell the news outlets that the Spirit of New Orleans will be released in a limited and exclusive launch very soon, and we'll be sending them bottles in advance so they can write reviews themselves." I pause. "Tell Jeff Doon that we're making arrangements based on best practices I learned at a distillery that conducts tours in Dublin, and as soon as we have all safety measures in place, we'll be ready to launch. Also tell him that we'll expect him to coordinate with the press so they're the first to experience New Orleans' latest attraction."

"I like it, boss. Making all the notes."

"Okay. Distributors—make sure they get the same press release, and tell them we'll start taking their orders in advance, but we'll expect partial payment to hold them as we expect to sell out of the first batches in a very short time."

"Ohhh. Ruthless. That's even better."

It's on the tip of my tongue to say I've learned from the best, but I hold it in. Instead, I take another moment to acknowledge how much Lachlan has changed me. The confidence I've gained in myself and my authority isn't a coincidence. He made me believe in myself, and that was just another chink in the walls that came crashing down from around my heart. I smile, feeling more like a CEO than I have since the day the desk in the basement became mine.

Which brings me to the next issue.

"I'll deal with Dad myself. I don't want him, my mom, or my sisters coming here under any circumstances."

Temperance goes quiet on the other end of the call. "Does this have to do with the other things you need to tell me?"

For a moment, I wonder at the wisdom of divulging what I'm about to share, but Temperance needs to be prepared. Based on what I know about Lachlan Mount, as long as there's a threat out there against him that could potentially spill over to me, there's no way he's going to let me go back to living my normal, or even a semi-normal, life.

"Yes. And I need you to swear on whatever you consider holy that this goes in the double vault. Sharing anything I tell you could quite literally cost you your life."

Temperance is silent for several long moments instead of brimming with the questions I expected her to shoot at me rapid fire. If I were her, I'd ask if I was calling from the mental health ward of the hospital and whether that's why she's been unable to contact me, but Temperance doesn't. Instead, she surprises me.

"I know you think that life is all black and white, Keira, but for some of us, gray is a lot more accurate. Whatever you're going to tell me won't go beyond us. I know plenty of things that could already land me in a crypt, and I know how to keep my mouth shut. This isn't the first time my life, or the life of someone I love, has depended on it."

Her answer may be nothing like I expect, but it's everything I need to hear.

"Someday, you're going to tell me what that means, but we don't have time right now."

"Agreed, boss. Let's get to what matters."

"I'm not going to be coming into the office for a little while."

"Now you're really making me wish we had a code word for situations where you've been kidnapped."

I can't help but chuckle at that, and my body twinges in protest. "Yeah, we probably do need a code word, but not today. I had a bit of an accident, and there's a security threat—"

Temperance interrupts, her tone panicked. "Accident? Are you okay? What happened?"

"I'm fine, but . . . the consequences of the accident are further reaching than just me. I can't tell you everything, except that I need you to step up and be my new COO. You need to handle business in person while I work remotely."

A harshly indrawn breath is her first response. "I'm reading between the lines here, Keira, and I don't like it."

I swallow, blocking out the aches in my body, determined to handle this like the boss I am. "I'm safe, and I'm certain that nothing is going to happen to me. But in order for that to continue to be the truth, I need you to do exactly what I tell you."

"Okay. I'll drop the questions. I know less is more. Tell me what you need me to do."

I spend another five minutes giving Temperance her marching orders, along with the raise I promised her. "It'll show up in your next check."

"Are you sure?"

"Yes."

I don't care that Lachlan's money will be funding the raise temporarily, because Seven Sinners is about to level up in the whiskey world, thanks to the very same man. Or am I just stepping up to finally be the leader he made me realize I am? *Another shift.*

"I've got what I need. Except . . . can I tell you to be careful? I know you're not giving me everything, but I'm picking up enough to realize that you're in some serious shit. And if it has to do with what I think, *please* make sure you know what you're doing."

"I've got this, but thank you."

She's quiet for another moment. "Okay. You better call your dad."

"That's up next. Thank you for listening . . . and reading between the lines."

"I still want a code word for kidnapping."

"I promise I'll throw in something about chardonnay or prosecco."

A laugh bursts from Temperance. "Then I'll really know you're in deep shit."

"Exactly."

When we hang up, I stare down at the phone, wondering how the hell I'm going to handle the next call.

EIGHT

Mount

"**W**HERE THE HELL IS SHE!**"

When I open my eyes and see the bed next to me empty and the unhooked IV line dangling from the pole, I'm not too proud to say I lose my shit.

The door bursts open, and Z and D rush inside.

"Where is she?" I demand, and both men recognize the quiet menace in my voice.

"With V. She needed to make a few calls. Business. Family."

My first instinct is to bend her over my lap and spank her ass for leaving without telling me, but I rein it in. A little. Leopards don't change their spots.

"Where?"

"Upstairs, because we're still under lockdown in here with no signal. Your order, boss."

V knows the penalty for anything happening to Keira on his watch would be death, and the man has proven his willingness to die for me. I expect he would do no less for her.

"Get her back down here now."

"But, boss. Ms. Kilgore told us we couldn't leave you unguarded. She said . . ."

When Z trails off, I prompt him to continue. "What did Ms. Kilgore say?"

"That she'd kill us both herself if we left you unattended."

A smile tugs on my lips. The fact that Keira is now giving my employees orders comes as a surprise. Part of me wasn't completely certain that the things she said to me earlier weren't a product of drugs, adrenaline, and shock, but it seems that I was wrong. Keira is stepping into a role I wasn't sure she'd accept, and she's doing it without any prompting on my part.

"And you believed her."

Both men nod. "She meant it, sir."

I let the smile free. *My little hellion.*

"Send someone up to let her know her presence has been requested."

The door, still partially cracked, opens the rest of the way.

"My presence has been requested? That sounds awfully official."

Even in a scrub top the color of a Smurf and two sizes too big, Keira still has the bearing of a queen. She gives the men a nod and they leave the room, shutting the door behind them as she comes toward the side of her bed closest to mine.

"Did you handle what you needed to handle?"

"Yes. As much as I could. I've delegated a lot to

Temperance. She's COO in my absence, and I guilt-tripped my father—without remorse, I might add—into not coming until I'm ready for him to come."

The mention of her father stops me cold. "Now is not a good time for your family to be in the city."

"I know. And they're not coming. Do you still have someone who can protect them? All of them?"

"Yes. They'll be under protection until I give an order for that protection to cease. Which I have no intention of doing. I made you a promise, and I'll keep it."

Keira pauses between our beds. I can tell she's running low on energy after walking around. I may be able to power through pain, but that's because I've never had a choice. She should never have to.

"Thank you."

"You don't need to thank me for that." I reach out and snag her hand. "Come here." I gently bring her closer as I move over in my bed, ignoring the pain of the gunshot wound.

"I won't fit."

"Bullshit."

Her mouth screws up into a stubborn expression, but she comes anyway, and we both get as comfortable as the bed will allow. Keira's face is inches from mine when I speak again.

"You said you wouldn't leave me, and here I am, waking up alone."

"Emergency. I made sure you were covered."

I shake my head. "That's not your job."

"Wouldn't you do the same for me?"

"It's different."

MEGHAN MARCH

Her eyes narrow on me. "No, it's not. I don't know what got us into this mess, but I do know that I'm riding it out with you."

Us. The word reverberates in my chest. I've never been part of an *us.* But the way she says it, and the way she has stepped up when the stakes are the highest, makes me realize that this is the only woman who could possibly stand at my side.

"You can order my employees around, but never to the detriment of your own safety. *That* is a hard limit."

"Fine," she says with obvious reluctance.

"I have another deal for you."

Her hand curls into mine, and I'm addicted to how she touches me so easily and voluntarily. "I'm ready to hear your terms, *Lachlan.*"

I smile again at her use of my name, something I'm doing altogether too often for my own comfort, but maybe someday I'll get used to my lips curving upward. Or I could just make the streets run with more blood and call it balance.

"Terms. Unless I'm unavailable, unconscious, or in peril, I deliver orders to my employees." When her mouth opens like she wants to protest, I continue before she can get a word out. "*But* I will make it clear that any order from you carries the same weight as one from me."

Her lips press together for a beat before she responds. "I can handle that."

"Second, if I tell you to do something for your own safety, you do it *immediately.* I think you realize that life-and-death situations are not out of the ordinary if you're part of my life."

"Understood."

Her lack of argument or debate pumps a new feeling into my chest. *Hope for the future.*

"Finally . . . I still call the shots in the bedroom."

Keira lifts her chin in that stubborn gesture I've grown accustomed to.

"Are you going to lie and tell me you don't love it?"

She shakes her head. "No. But every once in a while, I get to take control."

"We'll see about that."

This time, a sly smile crosses her face.

"One more thing."

"What?" she asks, her tone edged with amusement.

"Kiss me."

She bites her lip and leans in, skimming her mouth across mine, and I answer her with an equally light response. When I pull away, it's with the taste of her on my tongue.

"You're not giving any of *those* orders until you're healed," she says.

"When *you're* healed," I say, correcting her.

"Deal."

I inhale and release a long, slow breath. I don't want to change the subject, but it's time. Before I let myself get drunk on her and the possibilities of the future, I need to answer her questions and tell her the truth.

It's time to show Keira just how black my soul is, and see if she's going to run in the other direction.

Which is exactly what she *should* do.

NINE

Keira

"NOW'S THE TIME TO ASK YOUR QUESTIONS."

Lachlan's change of subject after our negotiation is jarring, and I'm trying to figure out why he's pushing it. But I don't ask. I have a feeling I already know the answer.

This is a test. The one that will determine whether I hold tight to my new realizations and the position I'm ready to claim, or whether I run screaming from the room.

At this point, I'm fairly certain if I demanded it, he would free me from our bargain. Something has shifted in him too. I feel it.

"Are you afraid I'm going to run when you answer them?" I ask.

"Is that your first question?" His tone is dry, but I hear the underlying message.

"Preliminary. Just want to make sure I understand why you're pushing this."

Lachlan's dark eyes bore into mine. "Make no mistake,

Keira. I'm not a good man. If you're expecting a virtuous answer to any question you have, you're going to be disappointed. Your first impression of me will always be the most accurate."

His statement dredges up that first impression I had of him in my office. There was fear, but there was also more. He commanded every bit of my attention, putting my entire body on edge. His reputation terrified me, but he exuded an energy that sucked me in before I even knew I was in danger.

Actually, that wasn't even my first impression of him. Because that happened before I knew who he was. The night of the masquerade. The night he changed the course of my life, and I was clueless about it.

My true first impression of Lachlan Mount was—this is the man I've been waiting for my whole life, and the one I want to keep in it forever.

So, no matter what he throws at me, I'll be holding on tight to that memory and all of the things he's done since to prove I was right.

"I can handle that," I tell him without hesitation.

"Then ask away."

It's almost like he's daring me to falter in my resolve, which just makes me more stubborn. Maybe it's reverse psychology. Maybe it's another mind-fuck. But I don't think so. I'm pretty certain this is Lachlan opening up as much as he's capable of doing.

"Okay. Then let's start with an easy one. Did you pay my husband to disappear and fake his death?"

There's no remorse when he replies. "Yes, but you already knew that."

"Did you kill him?"

Lachlan goes quiet, and I wonder if he's going to answer. After a few beats, he does.

"I'm never going to tell you whether or not I killed someone. Not because I don't trust you, but because I'll never put you in the position of having to bear that weight on your conscience, or be asked to testify about something I've said."

I chew on my lip because it's not the answer I expected at all. I figured it would be a cut-and-dried *yes*. But this answer is much more complex. His response is as honest as I could ask for, and somehow makes me feel safer than if he replied like I expected.

That's when it hits me—Lachlan Mount isn't just protecting my body. He's trying to protect my soul from the sins that stain his own.

A wave of emotion rushes over me as I absorb the realization. He says he's not a good man, but he's miles better than the one I just asked if he killed. There's no doubt in my mind about that. But I do need to know if Brett is coming back or whether he's gone for good. I need that finality. I need to know I can move forward without fear of my past coming back to haunt me again.

"Keira?" he says, his prompt telling me I've been quiet longer than I realized. "Are we stopping at question one?"

I shake my head the slightest bit. "No. I'm just . . . thinking."

"And?"

"I have to know if he'll ever be coming back. I don't need details. I just need closure."

Lachlan's face is solemn as he replies. "You never have

to worry about him ever again."

My insides are already a maelstrom of new emotions and realizations, and this adds a healthy dose of relief to the mix.

"Thank you," I whisper.

He looks surprised at my response. "Why would you thank me for that?"

"Because I never want to see his face again for as long as I live."

"You never will. Next question."

We're both quiet for several moments while I decide what to ask next. When it comes down to it, there's one question I haven't been able to reconcile at all.

The night I decided he was the only man for me, the one I've been waiting for my whole life, I still can't piece it together in my brain how that could have happened. It seems like fate stepped in, but I need to know the truth.

"How did you get my note the night of the masquerade?" When I first learned that it was Lachlan and not Brett, I cut him deeply when I lashed out, and that's not my intent here at all. But still, I have to know.

"It's not a *how* so much as a *who*," he answers carefully, and the possibilities riot in my head, my anxiety growing with every second that passes.

"Who?"

"Magnolia Maison."

TEN

Mount

WHEN KEIRA'S FACE DRAINS OF ALL COLOR, I WISH I'd been able to keep this knowledge from her, but I promised her no more lies. Besides, this is something she needs to know, regardless of how much I'd like to protect her from the feeling of betrayal no doubt charging through her system right now.

"Magnolia gave you the note? How? Why? I don't understand why she'd do that. You said you thought I was a gift. It doesn't make any sense."

I wish I had better answers for her, but I haven't had Magnolia brought in to get them. "I don't know what her motives were, but she definitely had one."

"But—"

Stricken. That's the only way I can describe Keira's face. I thread my fingers through hers and squeeze, not taking a chance that this could be a wedge driven between us.

"Magnolia's a madam. She rose to power by having the best girls and the ability to procure anyone for any reason."

"But why would she bring *me* into it?" Keira's tone is beyond distraught as her hand drops, along with her jaw. She sits up, wincing at a bite of pain, her legs over the side of my bed before I can stop her.

I want to wrap her in my arms and stop her from moving, especially because I hate seeing her in pain, but this is how she processes things. I've learned that, and I let her have her space. For a few moments, anyway.

If only I could spare her this . . . but I can't. She deserves the truth.

"She *knew* that the note was supposed to go to Brett. She . . . ." Keira trails off, and I can guess where she's going with it.

"She suggested you write it?"

Keira nods, as if at a loss for words, her confusion and emotions warring on her face. I want to make one thing absolutely fucking clear before this conversation is over—that I'm thankful as hell I got that note.

I reach out and take her hand, closing mine around it. "Look at me, Keira."

Her gaze drops to mine.

"Regardless of how or why she did it, getting that note was the best fucking thing that's ever happened to me. It put you on my radar. Without it, I would've never known you existed."

She swallows and nods. "That's not the part I'm struggling with. It isn't. I swear. I wouldn't take back that night for anything." She squeezes my hand.

Her words and tight grip fill me with another measure of hope for the future. We're stronger than this. Stronger than the circumstances that brought us together. Magnolia's motives don't matter to me anymore, but I know they matter to Keira, and I understand why she needs answers.

Unfortunately, I can't give her answers I don't have. What I do have is a little more information, which I hope won't cause her more pain.

"The note was delivered to me by courier, and I was intrigued. Magnolia said she had someone special that her anonymous gift-giver knew I'd like. She guaranteed me that I would never find another woman who would compare, and she was absolutely right. You are incomparable. Unforgettable."

ELEVEN

Keira

Lachlan's hand squeezes mine tightly. I take the strength he offers, even as I'm faced with the undeniable shock of Magnolia's deception.

Before this moment, I didn't know it was possible to be torn in two completely opposite emotional directions. I'm thankful Magnolia put me in Lachlan's path, but the stabbing feeling of betrayal is undeniable.

She painted a picture of a man who was scarier than the devil himself, and yet she pushed me into his path. She couldn't have known how things would end up. *Could she?*

I just . . . I don't freaking understand.

"I don't know if my best friend was playing matchmaker or whoring me out."

Lachlan squeezes my hand again and reaches up to cup my chin with the other. "Don't ever fucking say that about yourself. She played us both, Keira. Like a master. I told you she's the best at what she does for a reason. She knew me. Knew what I liked, maybe even better than I knew myself.

Then she put you in my path—the one woman she knew I'd want more of immediately. You were the ultimate drug. She banked on me becoming addicted after only one hit, and she was right."

My mouth drops open again for what seems like the tenth time during the last few minutes, and not just because I felt the exact same way after that night. I wanted more. Needed more. Hell, I married the guy I thought he was the *next day*.

"I don't understand her motives, though. That's what doesn't make sense." And that's truly the one part that has me completely stumped. Was this another case of *Magnolia always knows best*? Or was she playing Russian roulette with my life?

"I wish I had an answer for you, but I don't. Magnolia Maison didn't get to where she is by doing things without a reason. She's smart. Cagey. I've always respected her. But you have to know one more important thing."

I brace for another confession that I'm not sure I'll be able to handle. "What?"

Lachlan's dark stare softens further, his thumb stroking my cheek. "Two days after the masquerade, I still couldn't stop thinking about you. About how fucking incredible you were. How you demanded what you wanted, and yet gave me everything."

His words send heat pulsing through me as the memories replay in my head, dulling the betrayal as I focus on what matters more—where I ended up because of it.

"I went back to Magnolia and told her I wanted you again. Long term. Exclusively."

"You did?" Shock rips through me.

Lachlan nods. "Of course I did. What you demanded and gave was completely unique. She achieved her goal. She knew I'd be hooked."

Confusion surges up again. "Do you think she expected me to start working for her?"

"I don't know that either, but when I inquired about terms and how to acquire you—"

When I wrinkle my nose at his term, he frowns.

"Hellion, that's who I was and what I did. Women were possessions. To be owned. Used. And put out of my mind as soon as my balls finished pulsing. I can't change that."

"I don't have to like that part."

His gaze bores into mine. "*Who I was, until you,*" he says, emphasizing each word. "I couldn't get you out of my head. You infiltrated my life. You changed *everything.*"

His confession soothes me, yet it doesn't change the fact that Magnolia lied to me. But that isn't Lachlan's fault, and I won't put it on him.

"So, what happened when you asked?"

"Magnolia said you were a one-shot deal. Out of the business. Needed some cash, and you only agreed to one night."

The tightness in my lungs eases a tiny bit. "So she wasn't planning to try to spread me around."

Lachlan shakes his head. "No. I may not understand why she did it, but I believe she was honest when she said it was a one-shot deal."

I want to believe that, but I don't know what to think about my best friend right now. I never would have thought her capable of this, so it's hard to trust anything else about her in this moment.

"How can you be so sure?"

"Because I offered her a fortune for another night, and she still said no."

Again, the words of a man I used to fear alleviate the pain of betrayal from this foundation-rocking confession.

Then it occurs to me why Magnolia had no choice but to turn him away.

"She couldn't give you another night because I eloped with Brett. I married him the next day based on what happened at the masquerade. Thinking you were him. The one impulsive decision of my life—"

Lachlan sucks in a breath. "I wish I'd gone to her that morning. You would've been mine from that night forward. When she told me you'd married another man and were beyond my reach—*not part of our world* is how she put it—I was furious."

"I never would've married him if I'd known—"

His other arm wraps carefully around my waist, and he draws me closer to him. He guides my face down to his lips. "I wouldn't have fucking let you. No way in hell."

His lips sweep across mine and I lean in, soaking up his warmth and conviction. This man changed the course of my life without even knowing he had. When he releases my chin, I meet his gaze.

"If you had to let me go because of Brett, then how did this," I gesture between him and me, "happen?"

Lachlan's face contains more pride than apology. "*Nothing* is beyond my reach, Keira. Nothing."

I have to force myself not to smile at his arrogance. In this maelstrom of emotion and confusion, one thing is absolutely clear—Lachlan Mount hasn't wavered at all about what he wanted. Which was me.

The pieces start to snap together.

"So you . . . you made this happen. Everything from then on was you pulling the strings."

"Of course. When the prize is right, no amount of effort is too much."

I can't even hold it against him. How else would he have gotten me to fall in love with him? I can't envision another path that would have led to where we are. Which makes this all the more confusing.

I think of how Magnolia told me to stand up for myself and not let him walk all over me. How I had to hold my own. Did she know it would keep his interest locked on me? Everything she ever told me is now called into question. While I'm contemplating this, Lachlan keeps going.

"I forced her to give me your name. I tracked you down, found out who you married. Started watching you that day. Did my research. Learned Brett's weaknesses. Learned he conned you. And then I waited . . ."

He trails off, leaving me desperate to know where he's going with this.

"Waited for what?"

"For you to realize exactly what he was on your own. I forced myself to stand back until you moved to sever ties."

"Why would you wait? That doesn't seem like you at all." I'm trying to come up with an explanation for it, but I can't.

"Maybe not normally, but you were different." He tilts his head.

Still confused, I ask, "Because you needed me at my weakest to swoop in?"

He shakes his head. "No. I wanted you at your *strongest.*"

"But I was falling apart—"

"No, you weren't, Keira. You were coming into your own. Don't tell me it didn't take a hell of a lot of courage to make the decision to end it."

I blink twice. *He's right.* Choosing to end my marriage wasn't something I did lightly. I struggled and agonized over the decision. Even with as short as my marriage was, it still hurt like hell to admit how wrong I'd been.

"So you watched and waited. Which explains how you knew the perfect timing. When I went to a lawyer. Got the apartment. Set things in motion." I press two fingers to my temple as more pieces slide into place. If I didn't already have a headache, this realization would have given me one. "And that piece of shit agreed to take the money and walk, knowing that you'd come after me for it."

Lachlan doesn't try to deny it. "I did what I had to do to get what I wanted."

"So this whole thing, from the very beginning, had nothing to do with the money . . ." My words come out awed at this ground-shifting realization.

He lifts a hand to tuck an errant strand of hair behind my ear.

"No, Keira. This has only ever been about you."

TWELVE

Keira

"THIS HAS ONLY EVER BEEN ABOUT YOU."

The way he says it sends tremors rippling through my body, but not in fear. Never again in fear. They're from something else entirely—the certainty that no one has ever wanted me like this man wants me. He admitted it himself. I was his addiction. He could have swooped in with his hood and his henchmen and taken me to his compound the day he found out I married Brett, but he didn't.

Lachlan Mount isn't just ruthless—he's a study in perseverance. He said Magnolia was canny, but he's a master strategist. I can't fault the outcome, but I have to recognize the fact that I was just a moving piece in a bigger game than I realized.

"You were playing chess with my life, and I didn't even know I was on the board." There's no anger behind my statement. I'm still just trying to understand this enigma of a man.

"Life is a chess game, Keira. Every single fucking day, you make moves that determine your future."

"And Magnolia turned me into a pawn."

"No." Lachlan shakes his head slowly, once again caressing my cheek. "That's where you're wrong, hellion. You've never been a pawn. You've been the queen from day one. The most powerful piece on the whole fucking board."

"What?" Suddenly I wish I paid more attention to the game of chess when my dad tried to teach me as a kid.

"A king has the most value, but without a queen, he's a hell of a lot less powerful. Together, they have the best chance of victory." He pauses, stroking my cheek again like I'm the most precious thing he's ever touched. "I've spent my life avoiding any attachments because I thought they would create a weakness my enemies could exploit. I didn't realize how wrong I was until you. You give me strength, and I swear to God, I'll never let anyone take you from me."

The vehemence in his tone should scare me, but I find it comforting. And then he says something that hits me even deeper.

"And while I'd never let anyone take you from me, right now I'm offering you a chance to ask all your questions. Pass your judgment. Make your own decision. I need to know if you can handle life by my side, Keira, because if you can't, I have to find some way to let you go."

The very suggestion tears at my heart in a way I didn't know was possible, bringing a sting behind my eyes at the thought.

"If you have another question, ask it now."

My brain is swirling a million miles an hour, and I can't

think of anything else that would change my mind. Not now.

Except . . .

I press a hand to my lips as I recall that first brutal story Magnolia told me about him. How he forced a woman to dance on broken glass until she slit her own wrists. I can't reconcile that rumor with the man before me. What's more, I don't want to even give voice to the possibility it could be true.

Lachlan must see the confusion on my face as he releases his hold on me. "Ask your question, Keira." It's a command.

I heave out a breath, gathering my courage. I don't know what I'll do if I'm wrong and it's true. "Magnolia told me a story about you . . ."

His expression goes blank, and a hardness infiltrates his features. It's that granite mask I can't stand to see on his face. It's like he's expecting the worst, and maybe he is.

"There are a lot of stories about me. You'll have to be more specific. Some are fact, and some are rumor and myth."

I just have to blurt it out. That's the only way. So I go for it. "The story about the woman being forced to dance on broken glass. Is it true?"

His expression doesn't change as he shifts away from me, and now the small distance between us feels like the Grand Canyon.

"It's true."

THIRTEEN

Mount

I SHUT MY EMOTIONS DOWN, ONE SECOND AT A TIME, preparing for the inevitable. The moment when Keira says she can't be with a monster like me. I *am* the devil himself, and there's no way she could want to be with someone capable of the things I've done.

It will shred everything left of my humanity to let her go, but I won't keep her trapped against her will. Not now. We're beyond that. If she says she wants to leave, I won't stop her.

All remaining color drains from her face, and the glimmer of distress that flashes in her gaze guts me.

I don't want her fear, but how could a man like me deserve anything else?

Heavy moments of silence hang between us until Keira, the queen I never knew I needed until we were both tricked into something we didn't see coming, finds her voice.

"Tell me why."

It's not a question. It's a demand, and one I didn't expect

her to make. I didn't expect her to care about the reason behind it.

"Does it matter?"

Her nod is infinitesimal, but I catch it.

"It matters more than anything I've ever asked you. Please tell me why you would do something like that. I have to believe there was a reason." The threat of tears underlies her tone, and I'd rather take another bullet than hear her sound like that again.

I don't justify my actions to anyone. Ever. But I know this is one exception I have to make, or I'll lose her forever.

I look away, not wanting to see her face as I tell the story.

"About ten years ago, there was a boy who tap-danced on street corners of the Quarter, near Jackson Square. I'd see him almost every time I left here. The same boy, day after day after day. People think that when you're the boss, you don't notice details, but that's completely wrong. When you hold power like I do, you know details are the difference between life and death. This wasn't one of those details. It should've meant nothing to me that I saw the same kid every day, but something about it twisted up my gut."

I pause, remembering the expression on the kid's face, and I force myself to continue. "Every time I saw him, he was more erratic. He should've been in school, or so I assumed. He couldn't have been older than six or seven. I wasn't sure. But he was more skin and bones than anything else."

Keira sucks in a horrified breath at the picture I've painted, but I don't look at her. I'm too lost in the memory.

"One day, I finally stopped and sat on a bench for six

hours, watching him with his bucket in front of him where tourists would toss their dollars. Every couple hours, a man or a woman would crawl out of the gutters and empty it, and the kid would keep dancing. I've been around long enough to recognize addicts of every kind. Meth addicts aren't hard to spot."

"Oh my God," Keira whispers, because she's catching on to where this story is headed.

I keep my eyes fixed over her shoulder on the far wall of the room, because the rage that builds inside me when I remember isn't something I want her to see.

"Please tell me they didn't . . ." She trails off, and I wish I could tell her that this story isn't going where she thinks.

"The high from glass, a more potent form of meth, can last for eight to twenty-four hours. When he'd start to slow down, they'd grab the bucket and carry him off for a little while. I followed them that day and watched as the woman, his *fucking mother*, would feed it to him."

A sob tears from Keira's throat. "No. How could she?"

"There are plenty of parents who do horrible things to their children, and there's no way to save them all."

"I can't even fathom—"

"You shouldn't have to. That kind of shit shouldn't fucking happen, but it does."

"So, what did you do?"

"I called a few of the crew. We grabbed the kid, the mother, and the asshole who was her piece-of-shit boyfriend and dealer." I drag my gaze from the wall and meet Keira's horrified expression as I confess just how fucking brutal I can be without remorse. "She made her kid dance on glass, and that's what she earned for herself."

Keira holds a fist to her mouth like she's struggling not to vomit, and I don't blame her.

"Street justice isn't a slap on the wrist or a few days in jail. Street justice is more than an eye for an eye. It's harsh. It's brutal. That's who I am, Keira. Harsh. Brutal. Without remorse."

The disgust on her face makes me wish for a single moment that I had been born a different man. A man who deserves her. But I wasn't. I was forged in the fires of the hell I grew up in. I survived the streets the only way I knew how, by climbing the ladder up Johnny Morello's organization.

I tear my gaze away from her, expecting her to run for the door. Instead, she asks me a quiet and unexpected question.

"What was the boy's name?"

"Rubio."

I study the white sheet tangled in my fist, keeping my attention anywhere but on her. Still, she doesn't run.

"What happened to him?"

I force myself to loosen my grip and keep my tone emotionless. "I made sure he was adopted by a good family. A family that would never hurt him again, because they knew what the penalty would be. I pay for him to go to a private school. He gets straight As. He's already being scouted by D-1 schools for basketball, but he can go anywhere he wants, and he knows that."

Keira's hand covers mine, and I jerk my head up to look at her.

"You saved him," she whispers.

"I watched his mother slit her own wrists." My tone is harsh, just like me. "Don't you dare make me out to be some kind of hero, because that's the last fucking thing I am."

Keira's green gaze turns flinty. "I don't need a god-damned hero, Lachlan. I need a man who isn't afraid to stand up for the people who can't defend themselves. You can call it whatever you want, but I call it justice and honor."

I narrow my gaze on her. "You're missing the point."

She shakes her head, her stubborn chin rising another inch in challenge. "No, you're missing the point. You don't see it, but I do. I'm willing to bet everything I have that this kid isn't the only one you've saved from a fate worse than death. How many other innocents have you exacted retribution for?"

Eighteen years earlier

Boss had sent me on a run to meet with one of the old guard, a former top cartel leader set up by the CIA in a cushy house in the Garden District as his retirement package. Anyone who thought the drug trade was started solely by those south of the border needed to look a hell of a lot closer to home. The war on drugs is a joke because it's a war we started, and one that'll never end.

I was supposed to drop off a package and pick one up in return. An exchange of cash for information.

One thing I'd learned from Johnny Morello was that information could be priceless. For the last ten years, I'd climbed the ladder of his vicious organization. Once you were in, the only way out was a body bag. But since I had nowhere else to go, I was content to shovel shit and haul myself up, rung by rung.

Now, I was in a position of trust. Morello took a shine to me for some reason I'd never understand. I was being groomed. I knew it. Everyone else knew it. And, apparently, so did this old man sipping tequila in his garden like he had all the time in the world and I didn't have somewhere else to be.

"You have the package?" I asked him for the second time. Like Morello, I didn't repeat myself often.

"Sit. I don't like your hovering." The old man's English was still accented, and I had to wonder what he traded to the Feds for this sweet setup.

I took the chair across from him, my fingers thrumming against the Italian wool of my suit pants. You'd think in the New Orleans heat, I'd be sweating, but Morello's tailor, Giorgio, only used the finest, lightest fabrics.

If someone had told me ten years ago that I'd wear a suit more often than ripped and stained undershirts, I would have laughed. I also would have been wrong. Five years ago, after I'd proven my loyalty to his satisfaction, Morello brought me into his inner circle, and Giorgio made me my first ever suit.

The feel of silk against my skin was one I never thought I'd get used to, but now, it was second nature. I finally understood why the men who wore suits seemed more confident and in control. Because that was exactly how I felt the first time I looked at myself in the mirror. That was also the day Morello hired a tutor to teach me to stop talking like the street kid I'd been, and how to sound like I had an education beyond blood and survival.

"You seem like a smart man, Mr. Mount. Morello has

been grooming you to become his second-in-command, has he not?"

"Sir, respectfully, I'm here for the package. I have somewhere to be."

The old Mexican shook his head. "I will never get used to some of your American ways. In my culture, things are different."

"Here, we don't have all the time in the world to wait around. At least, not in Mr. Morello's organization."

The old man reached for the envelope beside him, one that held the information we were purchasing in order to seize control of the drug supply into the city to keep the cartel out. For now, anyway. I was smart enough to see the writing on the wall. Their power would continue to grow, and eventually, we'd have to strike a deal with them. Morello probably didn't agree, but sometimes his arrogance interfered with seeing things clearly.

When the old man held out the envelope, I reached for it, but he kept it tight in his grip.

"Tell me, Mr. Mount, are you a good man?"

I reared back at the question. "What the hell does that have to do with anything?"

"Just satisfy an old man's curiosity."

I looked into his faded brown eyes and told him the truth. "No. I'm not."

For some reason, this must have pleased him. A smile spread across his face.

"I respect your honesty." The smile disappeared as quickly as it came. "But I do not respect your boss's. He rules with fear and intimidation. Not with respect. True power, and the ability to keep it, requires all three."

His statement hit me hard, and I recognized the truth of it. Still, I kept my face expressionless because I knew where my loyalty lay, and it wasn't with the old Mexican.

"Whatever beef you have with Mr. Morello has nothing to do with me."

The old man tilted his head to one side. "What if I told you that he likes his girls young."

My teeth clenched together. It was like this guy knew my triggers. "As long as they're legal and willing, it isn't a damn bit of my business."

I knew what Morello liked. The younger and blonder, the better. I'd done my due diligence, though, and I made sure they were all legal and that none appeared to be forced. I might not be a good man, but I did have limits.

"And if they weren't legal and willing?"

I shoved out of the chair and stared down at him. "Get to the fucking point, old man, because I'm not here to play twenty questions." The respect in my tone was gone, and so was my patience.

He nodded at my suit. "Your tailor, he has a daughter. She's young and blond. How old is she?"

The fact that he knew this kind of information gave me a hint of why the CIA pandered to him like he was a freaking king.

"What's your point?" I ground out the words, not liking where he was going with this. Part of me thought he was just fucking with my head to see how loyal I really was. Maybe this was a test. Maybe this was something he and Morello had concocted together.

"Keep an eye on your tailor's daughter if you give a shit about her. Because, apparently, legal is too old for

Morello these days."

The thought of Morello touching Greta—a fourteen-year-old girl, the same age Hope was when Jerry tried to rape her—sent the same kind of killing rage I felt that night through me again.

"What the fuck do you know? And why are you telling me?"

The old man shrugged. "Maybe I don't like men who hurt children. Something I hear we have in common."

He couldn't know about my past. That was impossible.

I ripped the envelope from his grip and tucked it under my arm. "Nice doing business with you."

"And you, Mr. Mount. I expect I'll see you again soon."

The old Mexican's words haunted me for days.

I turned over the envelope to Morello, but I said nothing about the accusations. Instead, I watched and waited. Hoped like hell the old man was full of shit.

When Morello sent Giorgio to Italy to handpick new material, an ominous feeling settled in my bones. Greta and Giorgio lived on the premises. Giorgio was a widower, and Morello had assured him that Greta would be looked after in his absence.

I was sent on run after run, making it impossible to keep an eye on her the way I used to sleep outside Destiny's door, and then kept watch over Hope.

I wanted the old man to be wrong, but my gut said he was right.

By design, I returned early from an errand, using the

secret network of internal hallways to reach Morello's office. It was the one room with no peepholes, and I entered without permission—a move that could cost me my life.

But my gut told me I had to.

I didn't want to believe what I was seeing. Morello's big hand was buried in Greta's hair as he bent her over his desk. His dick was out, and her shirt was torn. Her cries and his taunts filled my ears before the rush of blood took over.

I saw Hope and Jerry. Not Greta and Morello. The killing calm slipped over me, and I didn't stop to consider the consequences of my actions.

I pulled the gun from the holster that never left my side and silently crossed the room. With ice water running through my veins, I pressed the barrel against the back of his balding head before he could make another move.

"Take your fucking hands off her." My tone was low with harnessed rage.

"What the fuck are you doing, kid?" Morello demanded, his voice harsh. "Get the hell out of here, or I'll fucking kill you myself."

"Take. Your. Hands. Off. Her." I spoke each word deliberately.

"You're gonna die, kid. And I had such high hopes for you." Morello shoved Hope—I mean, Greta—away. From the corner of my eye, I saw her tearstained face frozen in fear.

"Tell me this is the first time you've ever touched her, and all I'll do is put a bullet in your head."

"Fuck you, kid. Don't you dare fucking question me. I'm gonna have your head on my desk as a paperweight."

"Greta?" I asked, not looking at her, but keeping my

attention and gun on Morello.

She sobbed, not answering.

"Tell me now, Morello. Make me believe you've never fucking touched her before, or *your* head is going to be the paperweight."

My boss finally stilled, realizing exactly how serious I was. "I barely touched the girl. She asked for it. Came in here begging for it. She wanted a taste of a real man."

"He's lying," Greta said, her voice breaking. "He told me he'd kill me if I ever told anyone."

"How many times?" I asked, my tone low and deadly.

"Every time Dad leaves."

"Don't listen to that stupid cunt. She just wants attention like—"

I cocked the hammer on the revolver, and Morello went silent.

"You're going to wish I pulled this trigger by the time I'm done with you. Greta, get the hell out of here. Go to your room and lock yourself inside. Don't let anyone in."

She scrambled to her feet and dashed for the door, fumbling at the handle, which I now realized was locked.

The old Mexican was right. I didn't care why he wanted me to kill Morello, but he knew I would. I was being played, but that was the least of my worries.

Keeping the gun to the back of Morello's head, I palmed the wicked-sharp six-inch switchblade in my pocket. It had spilled plenty of blood for him, and now it was going to spill his.

"You're going to die slowly, you fucking piece of shit."

"You'll be next, Mount."

I pressed the button and the blade slid out. When

I jammed it into one of his kidneys, Morello squealed in pain.

"No. That's where you're wrong, Morello. Because I'm taking over. As of today, this organization is mine. Anyone who disagrees will die just like you." I yanked out the blade and shoved it into his other kidney, blood already darkening his otherwise pristine suit.

This wouldn't be quick or pretty.

When I finished with Morello, his severed head sat on the corner of his desk, on top of a stack of papers. The rest of him sat in a chair across the desk from me. The visitor's chair, not the boss's. Then I called in each of the top members of the organization to tell them about the changing of the guard.

Revolution is not without bloodshed, and neither is vengeance.

FOURTEEN

Keira

Present day

I SEE IT IN HIS FACE—HE'S EXPECTING ME TO REJECT HIM and everything he is. But Lachlan Mount doesn't know me as well as he thinks, and apparently, I didn't know myself as well as I thought either.

The story Magnolia told me made me sick to my stomach. The story Lachlan recounted made me want to vomit even more, but for a completely different reason.

I don't fear him at all. Not a single bit.

Finally, I'm starting to understand who he is at the most basic level. Lachlan Mount will never be a storybook hero, but I guarantee Rubio would call him a savior. I'm sure there are plenty of others who would as well.

Lachlan Mount lives by his own code, completely unapologetic about his actions, but that doesn't mean he lacks honorable motives.

"You deal out justice as you see fit, but I don't think

you ever hurt an innocent intentionally."

"Don't lie to yourself and pretend that me saving a couple of kids offsets everything else I've done. You couldn't find a soul blacker than mine if you dug into the depths of hell."

He truly believes his own words. I see it on his face, but I think he's wrong.

"You want me to say I'm repulsed by you? Then look me in the eye and tell me that you would sacrifice me to save yourself."

Lachlan's dark gaze goes wide before he reins in his shock. "What the fuck are you trying to prove?"

"Tell me." My demand is as rigid as the man beside me. "Make me believe it."

His face twists into a mask of disgust. "No fucking way."

The triumphant smile that tugs at my lips is probably as twisted as the feelings coiling through me, but I don't care.

"You'd die for me. You've already shown me that. You'd walk into a hail of bullets to save me from one. You wouldn't let the doctors touch you until they finished with me, even though you needed them far more than I did. If you want me to believe that you're a monster, then you're going to have to do a hell of a lot better, because all I see is a man worthy to stand at *my side.*"

Shock flashes across his face. "I fucking terrorized you. Don't make this out to be a goddamned fairy tale, Keira. That's sure as hell not what it is."

He looks away, and this time, I reach out and mimic one of his favorite moves. I cup his stubble-roughened cheek in my palm and turn his head back to face me.

"I don't want a fairy tale. I thought I had that once before, and look how it ended. I want *real*, and you're the most real person I've ever met in my life. You don't hold back a single one of your sins. What you do hold back is the motivations behind them, and those motivations make all the difference in the world." I pause, watching as a flicker of disbelief creases his brow, and then . . . hope, maybe?

He doesn't realize yet that he doesn't need hope. He already has me.

"You didn't terrorize me. I might've been a little terrified *of* you, but I wanted you just as badly, if not more. Magnolia was right about a few things, including the fact that you'd fuck with my head and make it go to war with my body. But she was wrong about what matters most. She told me I couldn't afford to let you get to my heart. The truth is, I can't afford not to, because it would be my biggest regret. It's already yours whether you want it or not."

Lachlan's eyes close for a single beat. When they open again, it's like I'm staring at a different man. "Thank Christ, because I have no fucking clue how I could force myself to let you go."

"I wouldn't let you."

"I don't deserve you."

He believes what he says. I don't know if I'll ever be able to change his mind, but I'm going to do everything I can to show him he's wrong.

I lean in closer to him. "Luckily, that's not up to you. It's up to me, and I've already made my decision."

His arms slide around me. Carefully, mindful of our

injuries, he guides me back into bed beside him and holds me against his battle-scarred body. My cheek to his chest. His chin resting on the top of my head.

Lachlan Mount may think he's a cold-blooded monster, but I hear and feel the steady rhythm of his heart beating against my ear as I drift off into sleep.

FIFTEEN

Mount

As Keira's breathing slows to an even pace, her words play on repeat in my head. For all the sins I've committed, I don't deserve this woman, but I'm not giving her up. I'm not that honorable, even though she seems to see something in me I don't. Hell, after the story I told her, there's no way she should be sleeping peacefully in my arms. But here she is. Maybe, just maybe, there's some truth to what she believes.

The lives I've taken are many. And before mine ends, I know I'll take even more.

But something she said resonates with me.

"You're the most real person I've ever met in my life. You don't hold back a single one of your sins. What you do hold back is the motivations behind your actions, and those motivations make all the difference in the world."

I'm not going to lie and say that all my actions have noble motives, but most of them have reasons that I consider completely justifiable, not that I've ever felt the need to justify them to anyone, including myself. Remorse isn't something I feel. Some people need killing, and I have no problem being the man for the job.

For Keira, I should wish I've been a better man, but I can't put any power behind that thought. If I were anyone other than exactly who I am, I wouldn't be holding her in my arms right now.

I've walked through the shitstorm life threw at me, and I'm beginning to believe she's the reason. She's my reward. I may have forced her into this, but she just gave herself to me willingly, and that's not something I'll ever forget. I'll protect her with my life and all the power I have at my disposal.

No one touches her. Ever.

⁙

I drift off, but like usual, I sleep with one eye open. When the door opens, I have a gun in my hand before I even realize I pulled it from beneath the pillow.

J.

I lower the weapon as my second-in-command enters. Keira continues to snore softly in my arms.

"We got ballistics back on the bullet we pulled from the car."

"And?"

J crosses the room and hands me the report. "Five-seven. Subsonic."

That caliber of bullet is a favorite of the cartels in pistols and rifles because the ammo is armor-penetrating. They're distinctive weapons. You can't miss them, and in

New Orleans, there's one particular cartel that flashes those weapons every fucking chance they get. Subsonic means they were trying to keep it quiet.

"Definitely a five-seven rifle," I say. "The shot came from the roof. I saw the laser sight. That's the only fucking reason I was able to swerve."

J nods. "Too bad you weren't able to get the fuck out of the way quicker, boss. Maybe then they wouldn't have had to pump so much blood back into you."

"Fuck my blood. They took Keira's, and for that, they all die. The streets of New Orleans are going to run red with it. Confirm who took the shot before we retaliate. Then we take them all out."

J's eyes widen. "All of them?"

I nod. "Every single fucking one. Get the confirmation on the shooter before midnight and rally the troops. We meet in the war room at twelve to make a battle plan, and then we roll out. We're going hunting."

J's lips twist into a cruel smile. "You mean, we're goin' killing."

I nod. "Go."

"On it, boss."

As soon as the door closes, Keira jerks awake in my arms, her lips pressed together, turning white. "What's wrong? What'd I miss? Is everything okay?"

I press a kiss to her messy red hair as pain creases her features. "Nothing. Everything's going to be fine. But you need more drugs. I can see it on your face."

She opens her mouth to argue with me, but I put a finger to her lips.

"This happened because of me. I brought you into my

world. Let me take care of you. Let me make it right."

"Okay."

I remove my finger and press a kiss to her lips, my side twinging in pain as well, but the adrenaline already rushing through my system suppresses it. I don't care if I need to duct tape over the stitches. Nothing is stopping me from getting my vengeance.

I meant what I said to J. For spilling a drop of Keira's blood, all their lives are forfeit. The second they fired on me, they broke the compact they agreed to in order to sell their drugs in my city. If they're smart, they'll be ready, but they won't expect a response this brutal.

They should.

There will be no mercy for the men who made Keira bleed.

SIXTEEN

Keira

LACHLAN LEAVES THE ROOM TO HANDLE BUSINESS, promising to be back soon. V's on guard duty outside the door. I'm left alone with my thoughts, at least until a man brings down a wireless router, a signal-extender thingy, and my laptop bag, which was apparently retrieved from the car. Now I can do actual work.

I should be wondering how Lachlan handled the police about the accident, but let's be honest—I don't care. My thoughts are focused on something completely different.

My best friend.

Or maybe *ex-best friend*?

What was in Magnolia's head when she decided to give Lachlan the note instead of Brett?

I want to think she was protecting me again, doing what she thought was best. But being lied to by your best friend calls a lot of things into question.

She told me his mistresses went missing. How could she have wanted me to be one of them? I realize that's one question I forgot to ask, but in all truthfulness, I don't need to ask it. Lachlan wouldn't kill an innocent woman, and I know down to my bones that he would never hurt me. *Ever*.

But still, Magnolia doesn't know him like I do. If she thought there was even a chance . . . how could she have done what she did?

She's closer to me than either of my sisters. I text them for their birthdays and send them a gift card. But for Magnolia's, I put in serious thought, just like she does for mine. A few months ago, I had her favorite restaurant cater an amazing dinner in her condo, and I commissioned a silversmith to forge these incredible silver chopsticks for her hair because she's been obsessed with wearing kimonos.

So, how could she gamble with my life so easily?

I can't stand to lie in bed anymore. The painkillers are doing their job, so things aren't hurting like they were. The nurse took me off the IV last time she came in to check on me, saying I no longer needed it. Now I'm free to pace back and forth across the room as I try to come up with some kind of explanation that would make any sense.

But I've got nothing.

Because of Magnolia's actions, I had the most incredible night of my life, but with the wrong man. Or, if you want to be specific, with the *right* man, but I went off and married the *wrong* one.

I remember how surprised Magnolia was when I told her what Brett and I had done. I thought she'd be all high-fives about my impulsive move, teasing me about finally pulling the stick out of my ass, but she just looked at me in shock.

Magnolia isn't stupid. I know that for sure.

Like Lachlan said, she rose to her position by being cutthroat, but I'm not her competition. I'm her *friend*. Is this a case of treating your closest allies worse than your enemies? I don't believe it.

I don't have any answers by the time the tech guy finishes getting me set up. As he leaves, V gives me a disapproving stare and jerks his head at the bed, clearly indicating that I should get back in it.

I turn in the direction of the bed where my laptop waits, but I make a statement just to be sure we're clear on one point. "I'm only going to sit down again because it's easier to work that way."

He responds with a predictable grunt before leaving me alone once more.

I stare at my phone and hover my thumb over my Wi-Fi calling app with Magnolia's contact info, wondering what the hell I can say to her.

Actually, screw it. All I have to do is ask her one question.

Why?

I tap on the icon and wait for her to pick up.

SEVENTEEN

Keira

"THANK FUCKING GOD YOU'RE OKAY, KE-KE. I heard someone tried to take out Mount, and there was a woman with him. That you might've been collateral damage. I've been freaking out of my fucking mind because you haven't been answering shit."

Magnolia's tone borders on hysterical, but I force myself to go ice cold, Mount-style.

"If I were collateral damage, who would've been to blame for that, Mags?"

"The fuckers who clearly have a death wish!"

"Bullshit. *You* put me in this position, and I want some fucking answers about what possessed you to give my note for Brett to him."

Magnolia goes quiet.

"What? Nothing to say? Thought I'd never find out?"

"Ke-ke . . ."

"Don't even try to deny it, Mags. He told me you gave him the note. You set me up." I'm off the bed before I realize it, pacing with the phone in my shaking hand.

Silence hangs between us, and the fabric of our friend-ship shreds further with each passing second.

"Please say something. I'm trying to understand, but you have to tell me why, Mags." My voice cracks on the last word. Even though I wouldn't take back where I am, her betrayal is too fresh and raw to approach rationally. "You've been a sister to me, and you offered me up on a silver plat-ter to a man you thought was pure evil. *What am I supposed to think? Why would you do that?*"

When Magnolia speaks, it's like we've changed roles completely. There's no emotion in her voice because it's all ravaging mine.

"You wouldn't listen to reason about Brett Hyde. The most logical, smartest woman I've ever met, and yet you were totally unreasonable when it came to him. I tried to steer you away but you wouldn't listen. He had you under his spell so tight, I couldn't get you free."

"You could've told me what he was!"

"Would you have believed me? Every time I brought it up, you went on and on about how he was your soul mate. And you were sure of it. Fuck, Keira. You were so god-damned happy, and I knew it was all a lie. But how the fuck could I just tear your heart out and stomp on it? You *are* a sister to me, and I had to find a way to make you see it for yourself so you would run the other way."

"And setting me up to have sex with a man I'd never met was the way you planned to do it? Are you insane?" I spin on a heel, my voice shaking as hard as the phone.

"You don't live long working street corners unless you develop your gut instincts fast and sharp, and you sure as hell don't rise to where I am without having intuition bordering on fucking psychic."

I jam one hand into my hair. "What the hell does that mean? You're avoiding my question."

"Stop your fucking pacing, Ke-ke, and sit down. I'm trying to tell you why I was willing to make the wager of a lifetime with one of the most precious people in my life."

I growl, hating that she knows I'm pacing even though she can't see me. I sit back down on the bed, but only because my head is pounding again.

"So, tell me. Tell me why you were willing to gamble not only my life, but my family, my friends, my employees, my business, *everything* on your fucking intuition, and then lie to me about all of it."

My stomach turns as I think about all the lies she fed me . . . and how I believed every single one of them like she spoke the gospel truth.

"I told you, you were wasted on Brett Hyde. And I watched Mount go through woman after woman, not a single one keeping his attention. The blood of voodoo priestesses runs in my veins. I may not be psychic, but when I feel something as strongly as I did about how Mount would react to you, I couldn't not do it."

"You played with my life!"

"No." Magnolia's cool streak snaps, and fervor intensifies her tone. "I was trying to give you a life beyond what you could ever imagine. You were born to be treated like a queen. You're everything that's good and loyal and true, and your strength shines through like the brightest fire I've ever seen. Every king needs a queen like you, even if they don't see it. In my gut, I knew that if Lachlan Mount got one single taste of what you had to offer, he'd be hooked."

This time, I'm silent. I don't know what to say to her. She was right, but I still can't get over how she played us both. Magnolia doesn't need me to answer, though, because she's not done.

"I was right. But you went and fucked it all up and eloped with that piece of shit who didn't deserve to breathe the same air as you. If I could've killed him myself, I would've."

"And why didn't you bother to let me in on your grand plan, Mags?"

"How could I? You would *never* have agreed to it. I've always done what's best for you. Always, even when you didn't know it or couldn't see it. I shield you when I can. I push you when you need it. I was setting you up to be the most treasured possession Mount has ever had in his life."

"A possession, not a relationship! What if he wanted to own me and then got sick of me and shipped me off to God knows where like the rest of them?"

"I told you how to handle him, and you did it. I. Was. Right."

Magnolia's conviction comes through clearer than anything I've ever heard. She believes she did this for me, and that it was completely justified.

"You could've been wrong!"

"I wasn't, though, was I?"

My free hand clenches into a fist as my head throbs. I want to strangle her right now for her self-righteousness and inability to admit she played with fire and could have incinerated my entire world. Even though part of me knows I should be thanking her, the other part, the part that goes back to childhood, can't get over her deception.

"Why keep up the lies? Why not just tell me when he came for me?"

"I did what I had to do. Just like I've always done. From sucking cock to taking it up the ass, to making sacrifices that rip me apart. Just like I'll keep doing. Tell me you wish I hadn't done it. Tell me you want me to take it all back. I dare you."

"I can't and you know it, but that doesn't make it right. Years of friendship, and then I find out from Lachlan that you've been lying to me for months?"

"Lachlan, is it now? Right there, with one goddamned word, you just proved that everything I planned came together like a perfect roux. You're calling the most feared man in this city by his first name. And why's that, Ke-ke? Tell me you're not in love with him. Try to make me believe it."

I want to tell my best friend to go screw herself, because I hate how satisfied she sounds. Then again, she sees the truth too clearly.

"I shouldn't even tell you."

Magnolia's laugh, harsh but clear, comes through the speaker. "Get over your fucking self, Ke-ke, because I will never apologize for what I did. You're right where you need to be. Sitting on a throne next to the man who rules this city. I don't have to hear you say it, because I heard how he swept you away to Dublin. That man is gone for you. I may be getting my information from the outside looking in, but I know I was right."

"And the ends justify the means? Is that what you're saying?"

"Fucking right they do."

A violent torrent of emotions swirls through me at her certainty and lack of remorse. I don't know why I expected anything else from Magnolia. She's unapologetic about who she is, what she is, and what she always has been. But there's more. There's *always* more when it comes to her. I want to believe Magnolia's motives are as pure as she claims, but I know her better than I know my own sisters.

"So, tell me, Mags, tell me you did this only for me and there was nothing in it for you."

That shuts her down for a solid three seconds.

"You really want to go there, Ke-ke?"

"We're already there, Mags. No more lies. No more hidden motives. The only way we survive this with some scrap of our friendship intact is if you tell me everything right now."

"Can't you just be happy that you've got a real man like you've always wanted?"

That's when I know I'm right. There's more she's not telling me.

"Now, Mags. Or I hang up this phone and never speak to you again." Even voicing the threat eviscerates me. It would be like cutting off a limb to lose her, even now.

"Fine. But don't you dare get all high-and-mighty on me. I put you first. So what if having Mount fall in love with my best friend made my life a little easier?"

And there it is. My brain spins at her confession. Even though I suspected an ulterior motive, hearing it packs the force of a Hulk-like blow.

"What the hell do you mean by that?"

"Use your brain, girl. Say your sister marries the prince

of goddamned England. You don't think you've just hit the jackpot right along with her?"

I laugh, or at least that's what the harsh sound coming from my lips should be.

Now it's all clear. Crystal, like the award that shattered and stabbed into my side. "You just tried to justify it as being all about *me*. You setting me up for life. But this was about *you* from day one. I was a pawn in your little game."

"You don't think I deserve a little easier time in life? I've seen and done things that would have you blowin' your brains out in seconds. You want to begrudge me the little bit of slack I'd get by association if you're with him?"

Guilt—slippery, slimy guilt—snakes through me. "You told me yourself you have no remorse for what you did, for the chances you took with my life, so don't you dare play on my sympathies after everything you've said and done."

"Don't be a bitch, Ke-ke. We both know I'm better at it than you."

"You're right. You are."

Magnolia muffles the phone and I hear her yell, "Hold on, I'm coming!" before she returns to me. "My appointment's here. I gotta go handle some *business* because that's how I make my livin'. You wanna hate me for what I did? Go right ahead. But don't you dare think I didn't have your best interest at heart. You're where you were meant to be, with the man you were meant to be with, and it's because of me. Now, I gotta go."

"Mags—"

"No, Ke-ke. I ain't got no more time to hear you throw your shit at me. I'm busy."

The call ends and I lower my phone, staring at it like it

just grew limbs. My lungs heave and my blood races as all of Magnolia's confessions replay in my head.

How is it that the ones we think we know the best are sometimes the ones we truly know the least?

I can't deny that her instincts were right, though.

Either way, Magnolia and I are not done with this conversation.

EIGHTEEN

Keira

TRY TO BURY MYSELF IN WORK, BUT I CAN'T. I'M STUCK on what Magnolia said and did. I spin around, midway across the floor I've been pacing for half an hour, when the door opens.

It's the man my best friend made sure I ended up with by using any means necessary. I want to condemn her for lying, but I'm having trouble with my righteous indignation. Lachlan wouldn't be mine right now without her intervention, but that doesn't mean my emotions aren't completely conflicted when it comes to her and her underhanded manipulation.

He steps into my path, closing his palms around my shoulders. Somehow, the simple touch calms my chaotic emotions by a degree.

"You should be resting, but you're in full hellion mode."

"You could say that."

"I take it you got your answers."

I nod.

"Can you live with them?" His tone is quiet, but not patronizing. I hear what he's not asking.

Does this change things between us?

I meet the dark gaze I've come to know almost as well as my own, including how it flares with heat, goes harsh cold, or turns flat when he locks down his emotions. Right now, it's somewhere in the middle. Cautiously resolved.

"It doesn't change anything."

The flash of relief is so quick as to be almost indiscernible, but I see it anyway before he carefully pulls me against his body, one arm sliding around my waist and his other hand cradling the back of my head. His lips press against my temple before he speaks, low and firm, into my ear.

"Good. Because I'm not letting you go now, regardless of how or why we got here."

I revel in the strong and steady beat of his heart and soak up the warmth of his body.

This man is mine. Nothing else matters right now.

When he finally releases me, I see a new intensity stamped on his face and ask, "What is it?" After the conversation I just had, I brace for something unpleasant.

"You're moving back up to our suite. V will take you as soon as the nurse checks you out one more time."

Our suite. Not his. Not mine. *Ours.*

"That's definitely preferable to this . . ." I look around the stark white walls and medical equipment. "So, what then? What happens? I know there's more you're not telling me."

His lips press together as he studies my face like he's memorizing it. "There's always more, Keira. There always will be. Some you'll know, and some you won't. But we're going to steal tonight for ourselves, at least for a few hours."

"What do you mean?" His statements seem like code, and I don't have the key.

"You'll see. Go with V. He'll bring you to me when you're ready." He lowers his head, consuming the questions that would have fallen from my lips with a quick, hard kiss. "I'll see you soon, hellion."

A smile plays on his lips as he releases me and backs away toward the door. His gaze doesn't leave my face until the last moment before he turns to leave.

What is he up to? I latch onto the question, grateful to have something to distract me from everything else.

The nurse gives me another dose of painkillers and asks me a bunch of questions to check my mental state, then makes an offhand comment about me not hitting my head as hard as she thought.

I follow V without protest as he leads me through the network of interior hallways that continues to astonish me. Instead of exiting into the suite, we step into the hallway from behind a floor-to-ceiling painting.

"I swear, this is the coolest place ever."

V almost smiles. *Almost.* It's more of a twitch of a corner of his mouth as we stop in front of the glossy black doors. He nods down, directing my attention to new hardware on the wall next to them. Some kind of high-tech device. A fingerprint scanner?

"What is this?"

He gestures to my hand and to the pad. Taking a wild guess, I lay all four fingers on the glass, and a light turns green and the door unlocks.

"Whoa. Upping security measures around here?" I

turn to look at him, and he nods. "Can you get in?"

He nods again.

"How many others?" He raises his hand and holds up his first three fingers. "So, Lachlan and . . ."

He doesn't answer, of course, and I decide that it doesn't matter as long as Lachlan trusts them.

When I step inside, V doesn't follow. He shuts the door behind me, and I assume he resumes his guard position outside the door.

Our suite. It's the same room, but it feels completely different now. It's not a prison . . . it's a haven. This is where Mount can be Lachlan, and we can hide away from the rest of the world.

The black, white, and gold furnishings no longer strike me as odd, but comforting, because the reasoning he gave for the color scheme is something so completely *him* that I can't help but smile.

Lachlan Mount is a man unlike any other I've ever met, and although he's not the first that I've called mine, I hope he'll be the last.

I turn in a slow circle and catch sight of a note propped up on a box on the table. My name, in his familiar handwriting, catches my attention.

What is he up to now?

I flip the paper open and see what's written inside.

> *Take the box into the bedroom.*
> *You have an hour to be ready.*
> *Trust me.*

If it weren't for those last two words, this note would

have felt like all the others. Commanding and cold. But those two words change everything, which is fitting, seeing as how everything has changed.

I pick up the box that reminds me of the one I found on the bed in my apartment, but my reaction is completely different now.

Last time, I called Magnolia because I was worried I'd find a body part of a loved one inside, but she talked me off the ledge. *Because she had plans for us.* I push those thoughts aside, determined not to think of her again tonight.

Tonight is for Lachlan and me. No one else.

I lift the box, testing its weight, and walk through the bedroom door as I try to guess the contents. But before I can even begin to speculate, I freeze on the threshold.

What the hell?

A ball gown lays spread out on the bed, the skirt hanging over the edge. The crystal-and-sequined bodice is one I know all too well, because it's the same ball gown I wore that fateful Mardi Gras night for the masquerade.

"What is he up to?" I voice the question to the empty room and lower the box beside the dress.

Memories of that night assail my senses as I drag my fingers over the bodice. Flashes of heat burst through my body as the details come rushing back for what seems like the millionth time.

I lift the lid off the box and peel back the tissue. On top is the mask I wore that night. Maybe I should be surprised, but I'm not. If he were able to get the dress, he could obviously get the mask.

I place the mask on the bed and unfold more tissue to find a replacement of the thong he snapped from my body before he showed me exactly who owned it, and a pair of gorgeous stilettos.

Saliva pools in my mouth because I'm beginning to see where this is going. We're getting a do-over. I don't know why, but I don't care either. If I had to choose one night I could relive over and over, it would be that one.

When I remove the thong and the new shoes, which are way sexier and more expensive than the ones I wore before, I find a note at the bottom of the box.

Say nothing. Take everything.

It's a play on the words of the note I'd sent the night of the masquerade ball, and my pulse hammers against my throat in anticipation.

Whatever he has planned, I'm ready.

NINETEEN

Keira

STAND IN FRONT OF THE FULL-LENGTH MIRROR IN THE bathroom and tie on my mask, staring back at a different woman than the one who wore it before.

The last time I knotted these silk ribbons, I was anxious, but excited. Hopeful, but fearful. Optimistic, yet full of doubt. Tonight, I'm filled with a confidence I never knew was possible, and it's not due to the final box that I found on the bathroom counter, although that contained yet another surprise.

It was about six inches square and three inches tall. When I opened it, I found a tiara fit for a princess—no, a queen—resting on black velvet.

"You've been the queen from day one. The most powerful piece on the whole fucking board."

I lower my arms to my sides and study my reflection. Even with a few cuts and bruises, I look like a queen tonight, and I'm ready for my king.

A smile, one full of confidence and conviction, crosses

my face, and I turn away from the mirror. I cross *our* suite until I reach the outer door and unlock it.

V waits patiently outside for me. When he turns, his eyes widen, and for the first time ever, a true smile softens his harsh features. I can't help but wonder what fate Lachlan saved him from, because I have no doubt that his loyalty springs from something I can't begin to imagine.

"I think I did okay in an hour, don't you?"

I don't know why I ask him. I already know that despite being a little banged up, I look good. My red hair curls in silky waves down my back, and the tiara rests perfectly on my head. Then there's the confidence I feel—it puts a golden shine on everything.

V nods and holds out an arm like a proper gentleman, and I lay my hand on it. He escorts me back to the floor-to-ceiling picture, and it slides aside when he engages the mechanism. He leads me by the hand up and down and around corners until another hidden door opens into a dimly lit room done in all gold and white.

It's a . . . *ballroom*, complete with more ornate versions of the sconces I've seen in the hallways, but also chandeliers dripping with crystal, lending a low, romantic light to the room. It's not the size of the *Beauty and the Beast* ballroom, but smaller, like it's for more intimate affairs. It reminds me of the interior of the Roosevelt Hotel, all gold gilt and marble out of another era. I can picture flappers dancing and drinking champagne with men in tails.

V lowers his arm and points toward one set of drapes that reach up to the ceiling. They're at least twenty feet long.

"Is that where he is?" I ask, nodding toward the drapes. I assume they hide some kind of alcove, if what we're doing is recreating the night of the masquerade.

V shakes his head, but lifts up a finger.

"One minute?" I ask, attempting to interpret his rudimentary sign language.

He nods again.

My heart, already thumping, kicks up as adrenaline rushes into my blood and I head toward the curtains. As I sneak through the small gap, the light turns into a rainbow of colors from a bowed window and a railing in front of it. It's some kind of internal balcony, offering a view of a glowing courtyard through stained glass, lit by the nearly full moon.

The stained glass turns this little refuge into something out of a fantasy.

What is this place? I grip the railing, listening as V's footsteps recede, filled with equal parts wonder and anticipation as I wait for Lachlan to join me.

I don't hear him. I never do. But my skin prickles with awareness as the curtain behind me opens wider for a moment before closing completely.

I bite my lip to stop myself from speaking, and lock my fingers around the railing to keep myself from turning around.

No longer do I follow his instructions out of fear, but for a completely different reason.

Love.

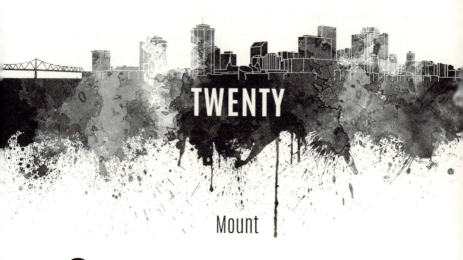

TWENTY

Mount

STANDING IN A DARKENED CORNER, I WATCH HER WALK into the opposite end of the ballroom. I lurk in the shadows, which is where I live my life, where I've always been content. It's where I belong. But Keira, she belongs in the light.

Somehow, I'll find a way to make this work, because anything less is not an option.

Her lack of hesitation, sure stride, and straight shoulders send every signal that this is exactly what she wants.

She has never cowered before me. Not even the first night in the library where she threw off her trench coat and defied me with that henna tattoo.

But this is different from not cowering. Keira Kilgore has finally come completely into her own. She's the most magnificent woman I've ever seen. Hands that have been bloodstained as often as mine have no business touching her, but I'm not letting her go. *Ever.*

I cross the room silently, a skill I acquired long ago out

of necessity and now employ for my own purposes. With a flick of my wrist, I move the curtain aside and step inside to where there's no shadows, no pale white light, but a rainbow of colors.

Maybe that's where we belong.

Not in the shadows. Not in the light. But somewhere completely unique to us.

I shut the drapes behind me, sealing us inside. Her muscles tense, but not like she wants to run. No, it's pure anticipation . . . at least, I assume so because that's what's running through my blood.

Despite my earlier injuries, I'm feeling no pain. Not when I look at her. I shouldn't take her tonight; I know that. I should wait until she's fully healed, but I don't have the luxury of time right now.

Tonight, I have to right the wrongs of the past and forge a new memory.

I step closer, drawn to the fiery red hair that matches her temper, loving how she stills in anticipation. Instead of being transported back to that night, the night she thought I was someone else, I stay firmly fixed in the present.

Because tonight, she knows exactly who I am.

I close the remaining distance between us and sweep her hair to the side, satisfaction filling me when I see the crown on her head. She deserves all the jewels, and likely has no idea that the emeralds winking in the white-gold setting are real.

No more pretenses. No more imitations. Everything from today forward is as real as it gets.

Keira Kilgore is *mine*.

TWENTY-ONE

Keira

GOOSE BUMPS PRICKLE ALONG MY BARE SKIN IN anticipation. When Lachlan's mouth closes over that *exact* spot, the one where my shoulder meets my neck, a moan breaks free from my lips. My nipples peak against the bodice of the dress, and my clit pulses wildly, enhanced by my piercing.

I don't know how my body can react to him so quickly, but it does. He barely has to touch me to set me on fire.

When he drags his teeth up the tendon of my neck, my fingers flex on the railing and I force myself not to let go. He nips my earlobe and I drop my head back, resting it against his shoulder. A gesture of surrender. Submission.

He tastes every inch of my bared skin before balling my skirt up and reaching around me to cup between my legs. A growl rumbles in his throat when he finds me already wet.

The sound that used to equally frighten and arouse me now causes goose bumps to form as he thumbs my piercing. I shudder as pleasure riots through me.

Any pain from earlier, including the headache that hounded me all day, has disappeared completely. I don't know if it's the man, the painkillers, or the sensations already flooding my body, but I'm ready for everything he has to give.

His palm slides up until his fingers wrap around the waistband of my thong, snapping it just like he did before. But this time it's so much better, because I know exactly what's coming.

Lachlan's hands close over mine on the railing, squeezing them tight, as if reminding me not to move them. I push my ass into the hard bulge at his crotch as my assent. And as a way to urge him on.

His hands are gone as quickly as they appeared, and then one finger spears inside me, stealing another moan.

The hiss of his zipper follows before the head of his cock nudges against my opening. He presses inside just an inch, and stills. I'm not sure what he's waiting for, but I turn my head just enough to meet his eyes, lit by the brilliant colors in a way I've never seen them before.

Maybe it's fate that I'm seeing him in a completely new light.

His gaze flares with heat as his lips cover mine. I'm still captivated by his stare when he pushes inside me, one inch at a time. Slowly. Carefully. But still filling me so full, there's no doubt to whom I belong.

Lachlan Mount owns me—body, heart, and soul.

TWENTY-TWO

Mount

UNLIKE ON THAT NIGHT THAT CHANGED BOTH OUR lives, I take her slowly, in absolutely no hurry, and with more care than ever before. Not only because of the injuries we both sustained, but because tonight is different, no matter how similarly it started. Everything has changed.

As her muscles clamp down, I finally let her push me over the edge.

When I pull my cock free from her body, I turn her around, letting the skirt of her dress fall as I fix my pants and lift my gaze to her flushed face. Her mask is askew, but that no longer matters. I reach behind her head and untie the silk ribbon to let the mask fall to the floor. I didn't wear a mask tonight, and hers was only symbolic.

I straighten the tiara on her head, and even with her mussed hair, courtesy of me, she's absolutely regal.

"Thank you," she says.

"For what?"

"For always giving me exactly what I need, even when I don't realize I need it."

I take her hand, threading her smaller fingers through mine, and lift it to my lips to press a kiss to the back of it. "We're not done yet. Not even close."

I pull her closer, taking her lips, something I'll never get tired of doing. I've never kissed another woman before her, and she's the only one I ever will.

No other man will ever kiss her. Touch her. Taste her. Feel her as she comes.

She's mine. And after tonight, she won't have any doubt.

When I release her and her eyes flutter open again, I lead her toward the curtain. There, I pause and ask her the most important question of my life.

TWENTY-THREE

Keira

"**D**O YOU TRUST ME?" LACHLAN'S GAZE TAKES ON a new intensity as he asks me.

How can he question it anymore?

"Of course."

He presses a kiss to my fingers before he draws them away. "I come from the darkness. I'll never be able to live with you out in the open. Being with me will never be normal, never be what you planned for your future. Ever."

"I don't care. I don't want normal. I just want you."

"I don't know why you have faith in me."

I reach out and grip the lapel of his jacket. He doesn't get it, but someday he will. "You don't hide who you are."

"I'm the devil in a suit."

I shake my head. He's so wrong. "That's what you think, but I can look beyond the surface to what you're hiding beneath. There's a beauty in you that you'll never see until you look through my eyes."

"Don't try to make me into some kind of white knight,

Keira. I'm not even close."

"No. You're not. But you're also not the devil. You're more like Michael the archangel. He defeated Satan. You've defended those who didn't have the ability to save themselves. You swept in and took vengeance. You keep the balance. You can think you're evil all you want, but I think you've driven out more evil than you've ever caused."

His dark gaze widens for a moment before he tames the surprise in it and sweeps open the curtain.

Lachlan leads me through the hidden hallways, his hand never leaving mine, until we stop in front of a fancy-looking security device that matches the one V showed me on the door to the suite. He presses his fingers against it, and the panel slides open to reveal the closet of our suite.

"Someday, I'm going to learn these hallways."

He smiles down at me, his face gentle. "Someday, you'll learn it all, hellion."

The door closes behind us, and he turns to face me.

"I told you I'd protect you, and I will. With my life and everything I have. This is the best way I know how. I have one more box for you tonight, Keira." His hand tightens on mine as he leads me through the bathroom and into the bedroom.

My heart rate picks up as his hand closes over the knob, and I repeat his words in my head.

Does he mean . . .

Before I can finish forming the question in my mind, Lachlan opens the bedroom door to reveal two men waiting inside the living room. Both are dressed in black, with the exception of one very distinctive white collar.

"Father. Your Honor. We're ready."

TWENTY-FOUR

Keira

Two days later

"WE CONTINUE OUR COVERAGE AS THE BODY count of known cartel members rises in New Orleans. The statement we've received from the police doesn't give us much to go on, except for the warning they want to share with our viewers.

"*Stay inside. Venture out only as necessary.*

"*Collateral damage has been minimal up to this point, and authorities want it to stay that way. Here at the network, we're not sure what to make of this, but somehow, even though the streets are running with blood, residents of certain neighborhoods claim that they feel a new sense of safety rather than fear.*"

The streets are running with blood, and I feel no guilt

over it. It's a simple matter of cause and effect. Actions and consequences. Restoring the balance.

Before all of this happened, I would have been one more scared citizen wondering what was happening to my city, but now I see it all from a different—and in my opinion, clearer—perspective.

Lachlan Mount isn't terrorizing this city. He's making it safer.

He hasn't contacted me. For days, V has stood guard outside my door during the day, and has slept inside the living area, probably with one eye open, while I'm in the bedroom at night.

I'm in the safest place I could possibly be, under the watchful eye of a devoted protector.

Now I just need Lachlan to come home.

In the meantime, I try to distract myself with work.

My phone rings at the prescribed time.

Temperance.

"Hey. Everyone still good?"

"Yes. I have everyone non-essential working from home like you requested. The restaurant is still closed, and the security detail patrolling the building makes the rest of us feel like we've got the National Guard protecting us. I don't know where you found the money for that, but . . . I'm really glad you did."

I rub a hand over my face, debating once more whether I should tell her the truth, but decide that the less she knows, the better. At least, for now. "If you think, for a single second, that you or anyone else at the distillery is in danger, we shut down operations completely and everyone evacuates according to the plan."

"Boss, we're not shutting down. We're not pussies here at Seven Sinners. It's going to take a hell of a lot more than a few bullets flying outside to stop us from making whiskey. Besides, we keep getting more requests for orders and I'm holding them off, because there's no way we can possibly fill them all."

My brain, which has been filled with constant worry about Lachlan's safety to the point where I've almost worn a path in the carpet of the bedroom, finally latches onto business fully once more. "Supply and demand. We have to raise prices."

Temperance is silent for a few beats. "Why didn't I think of that?"

"You would've. Things have been a little hectic," I say, and we both laugh at the understatement of the year.

We discuss how to handle the price increase, and then Temperance moves on to the next topic.

"I just got a call from the PR director of the Voodoo Kings, and he's concerned that Mardi Gras will be too dangerous this year because of the increased violence. They're already discussing the possibility of canceling the event, even though we're still months away. I told him that he was being unreasonable. I think I convinced him that there's no need for such a hasty reaction, but you might need to step in and make sure."

"They can't cancel."

"That's what I told him, but if they do . . ."

My mind races, and I think of the contract. "Hold on. Let me pull up the termination clause. Didn't we put something in there about forfeiting the deposit if they cancel within a certain number of days of the event?"

I remember the lawyer mentioning something, but I was barely paying attention because I was more worried about getting the damned thing signed than the details.

"Yes! Yes, we did!" Temperance says, excitement in her voice.

I pull up my own copy and read through the fine print, then check the calendar.

"They're within the window. They would lose the entire fifty-percent deposit if they cancel now." Relief—sweet, sweet relief—bubbles up in my belly. "There's no way they're going to want to pay for half a party they're not getting, will they?"

"No, ma'am. Do you want me to call and remind them, or do you?"

I think of my other options, continuing to pace the room. "I'll call them. Make it friendly. Pose it as *I would hate for you to lose that deposit just because of a little scare that can't last much longer.*"

"Do you have some kind of secret insight into how long this craziness is going to last?" Temperance asks.

"Of course not," I say, which isn't completely a lie. "But I can sure tell the team that they'd be making a poor business decision based on irrational fears, and would be much better off not losing their deposit right now."

"I'll let you handle that one, boss. I think it'll be better coming from you."

"Fair enough. What's next?"

"Jeff Doon wants to know if we've made any progress on prepping to start tours. But, obviously, he isn't pushing to start them right away."

"Maybe it's a blessing in disguise. We're not ready yet.

Anything else?"

"I think that's it for now, except . . ." Her question trails off.

"What?"

"Are you still somewhere safe? I can't help but worry about you."

I look around the luxurious suite, inside what's probably the most well-guarded compound in the city. "I'm safe. I promise."

"And there's nothing else you want to tell me?"

"Not right now. I'll be back soon, though. Like I said, if you think there's any question of danger, you have my authority to tell Louis to shut down operations immediately and evacuate the building. The security guys will take you home and make sure nothing happens to anyone."

"We're not going anywhere. Louis would sooner leave those stills than leave a newborn in the street."

How I earned such devotion and loyalty from my employees, I'll never really understand, but I'm thankful for it all the same.

"You're both getting hazard pay for this. Keep me posted if anything changes."

"Will do. Same to you."

When we hang up, I make the call to Mr. Joseph, the Voodoo Kings' PR director, reminding him of the termination clause they agreed to. After some sputtering and protests, and my assuring him that everything will be fine, he agrees not to cancel the event.

That's a victory for the day.

As soon as I get off that call, I start pacing again.

I can't help it.

I won't be able to stop until I see Lachlan again for myself, and with each hour that passes, I worry more and more.

TWENTY-FIVE

Mount

"**H**OW MANY MORE?" I ASK SAXON, LOWERING MY scope. In just under seventy-two hours, we've rid New Orleans of nearly every member of Eduardo's crew.

"Four. They're huddled like bitches in that compound." The hit man sounds disgusted at the cowardice shown by the cartel leaders.

"They've got you on their asses, so I'd expect nothing less."

Saxon tilts his head to the side. "True."

Keira compared me to Michael the archangel—which is eerie for its own reasons, given my former name—but we're not seeking any kind of divine justice here. Yes, I'm taking vengeance for every drop of blood of hers they dared to spill, but it's also full-blown retaliation for the cartel going back on their deal. You don't retain power in my position by making an example of one man.

No. You make an example of them all. Every. Last. One.

And when this faction is extinct in New Orleans, their rival will rise to power, but with a respect for my rules that's forged in the blood of their enemies.

We're making a statement, and it's not pretty.

I'm dressed in black, just like Saxon, wearing body armor and weighed down with more ammo and better-quality weapons than a marine carries into a firefight. We're perched on a rooftop over a half mile away from the cartel headquarters, doing our recon on these last four.

I've sent a clear message to Mexico that if they send one more man across the border, I will consider it an invitation to visit and bring an army. And when I say *an army*, I mean the best Uncle Sam has to offer from every alphabet-soup agency that I have in my pocket. This drug war could have been over years ago, but it's too damn profitable for both sides.

Another form lands on the roof next to us, and both Saxon and I have our weapons trained on him within half a second.

Ransom holds up both hands. "Go ahead, fuckin' shoot me. Then who's gonna make 'em disappear when you're done killin' 'em? The press would lose their shit if they knew how many more bodies the cops weren't findin.'"

Ransom's words are the truth, and Saxon and I both turn our scopes back to the compound. We left only the few bodies necessary to show we were serious and to get the appropriate level of media attention.

"You're getting paid. What do you care?"

"I'm not a fucking undertaker. I'm a smuggler. This is a waste of my skills. You better believe I'm upping my rate for body disposal after this shit."

I shoot a glance over my shoulder at Ransom. "You want to grab a gun and join us to break the monotony?"

He pulls out a wicked-looking long knife. "I prefer to get a little more up close and personal. Which general was it who said not to fire until you see the whites of the enemy's eyes? That's more my speed. Not this long-distance shit."

Saxon grunts, a clear fuck-you to Ransom. The two men might work together but aren't exactly friends, and they never miss a chance to give each other hell.

"I got movement," Saxon says, his finger sliding along the trigger of his sniper rifle.

"How the fuck can he see—"

Before Ransom can finish his sentence, Saxon has already pulled the trigger of the suppressed rifle. I watch through my scope and see a head burst into red mist.

"Nice shot," I murmur drily, and Saxon gives me the side eye.

"They're all nice shots."

Saxon's confidence is one of the reasons he's my go-to for any job requiring sensitive handling. He'd prefer to never work for me again, saying it leaves too much of a trail, but I couldn't give a fuck less.

I hire the best, and I pay him a fortune. He can deal.

One of these days, I know he'll disappear and make it so I can't find him, but it won't happen before this job is done.

"So that leaves three?"

Saxon nods.

"I'm sending the team in. It's time to make this even more personal."

TWENTY-SIX

Mount

WHEN I BROUGHT KEIRA INTO MY WORLD, IT BECAME my duty to protect her, including making sure she never knows certain threats exist. One of these assholes fucked up when he took a shot with her near me. Tonight, they pay and we end this.

How Ransom managed to get the gate combination to the cartel's headquarters, I don't know or care, but as we drive into the courtyard and under the portico, everything is still.

J speaks into the com. "Premises have been swept, boss. It's all clear. Your target is in the living room. Turn right after you walk through the front foyer. You can't miss it."

He is Eduardo, the man who sat in front of my desk and agreed to take over the dealings of coke, meth, and pills in the split of the New Orleans drug market. I was more than fair, but for some goddamned reason, he crossed the line. Broke the rules. Shattered the compact.

Now he pays.

The low-level shooter who put a bullet through the windshield has already been dealt with, and didn't say anything more than his boss ordered the hit. Now, his boss will answer for it.

Z opens the door of the armored Escalade and I step out. As I walk toward the door, I spy a pair of hedge clippers left by some gardener who probably fled days ago when the bullets started flying. Z follows behind me, and I nod to them.

"Grab those."

"Sure thing, boss."

I pull a Cuban out of my pocket and light it, taking a few puffs before I nod at him to open the door. Saxon, Ransom, and a whole crew of my best people are covering us from every angle. Not that there's anyone left at this point who could do any damage.

I step inside, my shoes echoing on the marble floor of the airy entryway, and head to the right like J described.

Eduardo is duct-taped to a chair and he's practically frothing at the mouth, spewing threats in two languages. Maybe three.

Regardless, I don't care.

"You will die for this, Mount. Fucking die. You and everyone you love."

I puff on the cigar, staring at him. "You're the one who broke the rules. I let you come into my city, make a shit-ton of money, and you dare take a shot at me?"

"I didn't fucking take a shot at you!" Spittle flies from his mouth as sweat drips off his face.

"Your man did. He admitted it. He said you ordered it." My tone is without emotion. There's nothing but ice in my veins.

"He lied!"

"How do I know you aren't lying?" I look over my shoulder at Z. "Get creative with those hedge clippers."

As Z walks toward him, Eduardo rails at me. Seconds later, his curses turn to screams just before his pinkie hits the floor. It's closely followed by his ring finger, which pings as the gold wedding band he was wearing hits the marble.

"Fuck you, Mount! You're gonna die for this! I didn't order shit."

I nod at Z again.

Screams fill the room, but all I can picture is Keira's face going pale as she fought to stay conscious after the accident.

"You do not fuck with me or mine."

"I didn't! He went rogue!"

"Then you should've had better control over your organization. For that, and the fact that you spilled even a single drop of my woman's blood, means that your life is forfeit."

I meet his dark brown gaze that's filled with hate, rage, and fear. What I've done to him is nothing compared to what he's done to others.

"I don't know what the fuck you're talking about, Mount."

I puff on my cigar again. "Then you've outlived your usefulness."

Z steps back and I give him a nod. "Put that piece of shit out of his misery. He's not worth my time."

I turn on a heel and head for the front entrance, curses echoing behind me before the distinctive sound of a suppressed bullet silences Eduardo permanently.

TWENTY-SEVEN

Keira

"THE TERROR RULING THE STREETS OF NEW ORLEANS *this week seems to have ended. Residents are still advised to use caution as they resume their daily activities, but bullets are no longer flying. The police haven't yet issued a statement, but we expect one to be forthcoming."*

With every hour that passes, I feel more and more like I'm about to lose my goddamned mind. The news stories online still have conflicting accounts of what's going on, but the tone has changed.

If bullets have stopped flying, then where the hell is Lachlan?

I've practically worn a path in the carpet from the living room to the bedroom in the last three days, but I can't even pretend to care. The only thing I want is him, back here, safe and sound.

Work is the only thing that has kept me sane. The distillery is still running at full capacity. Louis refused to leave, and the employees sided with him. They reminded me that we're built of tougher stuff in NOLA.

Temperance is a rock-star COO, so we've been able to handle much of the business remotely. But I definitely need to make an appearance soon, if for no other reason than to thank all my employees for their commitment to the company.

I turn to make another circuit on familiar carpet and freeze when I hear a knock at the door.

As much as I want to think it could possibly be Lachlan, I already know it's not. How? Because he wouldn't freaking knock.

It's not even quite noon, and I've already worn down my capacity for patience for the day, which means any distraction is a good one. I head into the living area to open the door and find V there with lunch.

"Come on in." As he steps around me to bring the tray inside, I close the door behind him. "Do you know where he is? Can you tell me *anything*?"

V sets the tray on the same table I've been eating at for days, and turns to face me. His expression is as unreadable as ever.

"Can you at least tell me he's okay? Because if I find out he's not and you all kept it from me, there will be hell to pay." I'm gesticulating wildly, like that will somehow entice him to reply.

He grunts.

"What does that mean?" My tone takes on a shrill edge, showing just how close I am to the edge and coming completely unraveled.

V points at the covered tray of food.

"I couldn't give a shit less about food right now, V. Just tell me—is he okay?"

He nods.

"Then where the hell is he? Is it over? I need to know *something*."

To this, he gives no response, sending my frustration soaring to record heights.

V begins to back away toward the door, but I stop him.

"Don't leave. Not yet. I'm going out of my mind here. Can you just sit and wait with me?"

His eyes narrow on mine, but he comes back toward the table and gestures at the food again.

"You sit. I'll eat. Okay?"

He nods and sits, removing the lid before pushing the tray in front of me.

My hand shakes as I grip the fork, but I barely taste the food as I shovel it down my throat.

We repeat the same process at dinner several hours later.

Still, no Lachlan Mount.

Where the hell is he?

TWENTY-EIGHT

Mount

DRAINED, I STEP INTO THE BATHROOM CONNECTED TO my office and strip off my jacket, dropping it on the floor. I glance at my hands, then turn on the tap and wait until the water hits scalding before I scrub them with soap.

No matter how many times I wash my hands, I still see the blood on them. Yet I feel no remorse.

I do what's necessary.

Fear. Intimidation. Respect.

That's how I rule my empire. That's how I protect my people. After the retribution we exacted over the last several days, no one will question my authority again, and only someone with a death wish would dare spill a drop of Keira's blood.

All the loose ends are finally tied up. A deal has been struck. And now life moves on.

Steam clouds the mirror as I turn off the water and grab a towel. Once my hands are dried, I use it to wipe away the haze on the glass.

I rarely look at my reflection. I don't need to see the devil staring back at me. But this time, I see something more, and it's not just the blood spray on what used to be my snowy-white shirt. No, it's a man with purpose. A man willing to make the streets run red if it means protecting what matters most.

Before her, I had every material possession, but still nothing to lose.

Now, there's nothing I wouldn't sacrifice to keep her safe. *Purpose.* That's what separates a strength from a weakness.

Keira said motivations make all the difference in the world. Maybe she's right. I'll never look into this mirror and see someone noble and honorable, but if that's the man she sees when she looks at me, I can live with that—as long as I get to keep her.

I strip off my remaining clothes and step into the shower, scrubbing every inch of me until I'm certain that not a drop of blood remains. At least, on the surface.

I'll always be brutal. Ruthless. Fierce in protecting what's mine.

She doesn't need to see that part of me. *Ever.* But I can give her the part of me no one else has ever had, and hope that it's enough.

When I slip into the closet through the hidden passageway, I'm silent as always. A glow comes from the bedroom, but everything else is dark.

My footsteps don't make a sound as I head toward the light.

Toward her.

She's asleep in the middle of the bed, her red hair up in a messy bun and her hand clenched around her phone, as though waiting for it to ring.

I should have called. Should have told her I was okay. But I'm still new at this.

I hope there's not a next time, but I'd be lying to myself if I said that. There will always be a next time. Another threat. Another person who needs killing.

But staring at the woman in my bed, I realize that I don't need to be the one exacting justice myself.

I need to be here. With her. Making sure she doesn't fall asleep alone, with dark circles under her eyes.

Everything in me wants to wake her, or at the very least, crawl into bed beside her. Instead, I take a chair in the shadows and watch over her while she sleeps.

My privilege and my penance.

TWENTY-NINE

Keira

WHEN I JOLT AWAKE, IT'S FROM A TERRIBLE DREAM. One where Lachlan never comes home to me because his blood drained down a gutter and his body disappeared, never to be found again. A nightmare.

"*No*," I whisper. "No. He has to come home." I wrap my arms around myself and squeeze.

"I am home."

I jerk my head in the direction of the deep voice, elated that the man I've been waiting days to see is seated on a chair in the corner. "Thank God. I thought you were dead."

I jump out of bed and rush toward him as he stands. In the dim light, I can see his face is set in harsh lines. *Mount*. Not Lachlan.

"I'm not dead."

"What's wrong? What happened? Are you hurt?" I stumble to a halt in front of him, taking in the pristine suit. What I really want to do is run my hands over every inch of his body to check for myself.

"Nothing's wrong. I'm fine."

I use that as an excuse to fling myself the remaining few inches between us, and his arms wrap around me and hold me tight to his chest. He doesn't wince, so I hope that means not only is the gunshot wound healing, but he truly hasn't sustained any new injuries.

"I was so goddamned worried about you. Next time, I need a call, or a text, or the freaking bat signal. *Anything.* V grunting and nodding isn't going to cut it. I need proof you're safe."

One big hand cups the back of my head.

"Bat signal?"

I breathe in his familiar scent, reveling in it and not caring that I sound like I'm crazy. "You're basically Batman, so yeah, a bat signal could be appropriate."

His chest shakes and I think he's laughing at me, but I'm not about to move to check.

"You know that's not how the bat signal works, right?"

"Don't argue with me, Lachlan. That's almost as bad as leaving your wife alone on your wedding night and not sending word that you weren't dead."

His lips press against my temple. "This is my first time as a husband. I'm pretty sure I'll fuck it up a lot."

Narrowing my eyes, I look up at him. "Rule number one—let your wife know you're alive, especially after you're done exacting vengeance."

Wife. I still can't believe I bear the title again, but it's true. I said the vows, and I meant them.

His dark eyes flash. "You're making rules now?"

I lift my chin. "Yes. I married the king. I feel like that gives me certain freedoms."

He grips me tighter against his chest. "I still can't believe you said yes."

I untangle an arm from his grip and reach up to rub a thumb along his freshly shaven cheek. "Of course I did. I'm in love with you."

Emotions fly across his face in wild succession, each one more vivid and intense than the last. "You can't mean that."

I meet the dark, burning stare that used to put the fear of God into me while stealing control of my body. Now, it infuses me with certainty. "You think I would've pledged *until death do us part* if I didn't?"

"You got my protection—"

I tap my thumb to his lips, interrupting him. "I got *you*. That's all I wanted. And if I have to spend the rest of my life proving to you that I mean every damned word, I will."

"I'm never letting you go. *Ever.*"

His vow holds the same conviction as mine, and I know we're going to be fine.

"Good. Glad we agree on that. Now, take me back to bed. We have a wedding night to make up for."

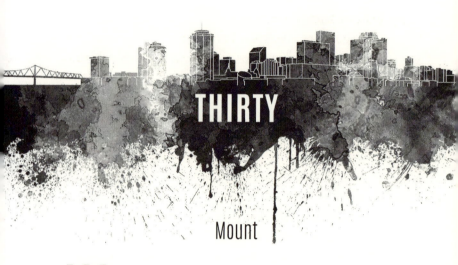

THIRTY

Mount

WORDS HAVE NEVER HELD AS MUCH POWER AS actions in my life. At least, not until this moment and this woman.

"I'm in love with you."

The fierce possessive instincts fueling the fire in my blood increase every time I repeat her words in my head.

I don't deserve to be loved. Not by her. Not by anyone. But that doesn't mean I won't take it. Keep it. Keep her. Protect her. Cherish her.

I've lied, cheated, stolen, and killed, and I will do it all again, especially if that's what it takes to uphold the vows I made in front of a man of God and a judge.

There's nothing I wouldn't do for her.

When I step toward the bed, I lower her down like the precious gift she is, but this softness won't last. The adrenaline from the last few days isn't something I can force out of my system.

I need to fuck my woman. Own her. Bury myself inside

her until we both scream.

Somehow, some way, she knows this.

Keira's voice is strong and pure when she speaks. "I can take anything you have to give. So, you better give me everything you have."

A growl rumbles up from my throat and I rip my suit coat off my body, flinging it away. Keira attacks me with the same fervor. Buttons fly as she tears open my shirt, and my hands go to my pants, stripping them away until I stand naked before her, ready to shred her clothes like she did mine.

But Keira holds up a single finger, pointing at me. "If all you had in the world is what you're wearing right now, I would want you just as badly. Love you just as much."

I don't know how to say the words, because I never have in my life, but for her, I'll learn.

Soon.

"I need you. Now."

THIRTY-ONE

Keira

ACHLAN TURNS INTO AN ANIMAL, TEARING MY SILK nightgown off my body. As his mouth ravages mine, my fingernails dig into his shoulders like they did that first night on the dining room table.

The feelings are just as intense this morning, but stem from a completely different emotion. He uncurls my hands from his shoulders and presses me back against the bed to kiss a path down my body, careful of my healing injury. He still sports a bandage, but he makes no indication that he feels any pain.

He drops to his knees before he pushes my thighs apart. "Already wet for me."

I open my mouth to reply, but what comes out is a moan instead as his lips close around my piercing. Such an unfair advantage, and one I'll never complain about.

Lachlan makes me scream over and over until my fingers are buried in his hair, tugging him up to my face. When his lips meet mine again, they taste like me, and I love it.

"My turn."

He shakes his head. "Fuck no. Can't wait."

He grips my hips, positioning his thick cock at my entrance with a fierce, possessive expression on his face. He doesn't hesitate, and I don't want him to.

One stroke. That's all it takes for him to fill me. He powers inside me over and over until his face contorts with pleasure and my inner muscles clamp down on him.

"I love you, Lachlan Mount!"

THIRTY-TWO

Mount

'VE LOST TRACK OF HOW MANY ORGASMS KEIRA'S HAD, but when she passes out limp beside me, I pull her body against mine and cover us both. We might not have gotten to have our wedding night, but I'll make it up to her.

I'm still stuck on what she said. Hell, what she screamed.

"I love you."

I've never known what the fuck the word *love* means. When you're raised without it, never feeling it, it's not something that makes any logical sense.

I already knew I would take a bullet for her. Die for her. *Live* for her.

If that's love, then maybe I'm finally starting to figure it out. There's no doubt I understand at least one part of it—I never want to lose this. Lose her.

I sure as hell never want to see her blood on my hands again. Ever.

She curls closer into me and I press a kiss to her temple, holding her tighter.

"They'll never touch you again."

My eyes finally slide shut. But instead of enjoying a dreamless sleep, I battle a nightmare in which someone tries to take her from me.

I don't know how much time has passed when I jerk awake, but Keira's eyes flicker open at the same time as I bolt up in bed.

"What? What's wrong?" She's instantly on alert, reaching for the side of the nightstand where a loaded gun is holstered.

This woman is perfect for me.

"Nothing." I grab her hand, pulling it back before she can snag the revolver. "Everything's fine."

She blows out a lungful of air. "Could we try waking up without the heart attack next time? That'd be great."

A sound grates from my throat, and I realize it's laughter. Or an attempt at it. "I'll work on that."

"Good."

"In the meantime, pack your bag. It's time to get the fuck out of town."

Keira's green eyes widen. "Why? I thought it was safe."

"It is. But I want you all to myself. Away from here. No distractions."

"Like a honeymoon?"

"Call it whatever you want, but it's time to go. I'll have the jet fueled and waiting in an hour."

Keira bites down on her lip. "I know this is going to sound bad, but please, understand where I'm coming from."

I brace myself, wondering what the hell could possibly put that uncertain expression on my hellion's face. "What?"

"I can't leave right now. I've been locked down for days, trying to run my company—that's rapidly changing—from inside these walls. And before that, I was out of the country for nearly a week without planning to be gone. And then the award, and a million orders . . . it's basically insanity at the distillery. I really, really need to go to work."

My first instinct is to override her protests and tell her that's ridiculous. She doesn't need to work. Not ever again. I have more than enough money to provide us the most lavish lifestyle forever. But I check my gut reaction.

"So, this is what it's like to be married to a CEO."

She nods. "I need you to be okay with this, because it matters to me."

"Compromise then."

Keira's head jerks back and her eyebrows go up. "You know what that word means?"

My lips twitch, and I think they're attempting a smile. "Only with you."

"Then I'll hear your proposal."

At her sassy tone, I pin her to the bed. "First, I fuck you. Then we put that last plug in your ass so you're ready for me."

Her hips lift up, grinding against me. *Yes, she's the perfect woman for me.*

"Is that all?"

"Then V takes you to work, stays with you, and you come home to me after you've got things under control. You have two days, and then we're leaving the fucking country again to go be Lachlan and Keira on a beach somewhere without another goddamned human being around for miles."

The smile that spreads across her lips is brilliant. "I can handle that."

"Good. Because you don't have a choice."

"I thought this was a compromise."

I shrug. "Close enough."

When I finally let her out of bed hours later, it's with an uneasy feeling riding me. Maybe because of the events of the last week, or maybe because of something else. As she gets ready, I step outside the door to the suite, and V spins to face me.

"Guard her with your life."

THIRTY-THREE

Keira

WHEN I WALK INTO THE BUILDING, I HEAD STRAIGHT for my office, hoping to get to the basement without anyone noticing my new bodyguard in tow.

I'm not sure why Lachlan has V sticking so close, but I'm not going to question it. My life has changed. I knew when I said those vows that I was stepping into a different world, and I would somehow have to figure out how to meld it with mine.

Temperance meets me at the door to my office, her attention going to V and then to me. "Chauffeur isn't staying in the car anymore?"

"Let's go inside. I need to explain some things."

V gives us privacy by waiting just beyond the door as I shut it, which is only going to lead to more questions from my employees. And this is exactly what I need to figure out with Temperance.

My new COO doesn't miss a beat—or a detail. Her eyes lock on my left hand. There's no way anyone can miss the massive oval diamond set on a thin band of diamond-encrusted rose gold. It has to be over five carats. I didn't exactly have the time or inclination to ask Lachlan how he found such an exquisite ring on incredibly short notice, because I was too dumbstruck by the fact we were actually getting married. Then again, he's Lachlan Mount. Things happen when he commands.

The whole event still feels surreal, as does the weight of another wedding ring on my hand. But this one, for some reason, feels exactly right.

"Whoa, boss. That's a hell of a rock. You rob a jewelry store and been laying low till the heat wears off?"

"Not exactly." The corners of my mouth tug upward in a secret smile, which happens more often than not when I glance down at the sparkling stone.

"When's the big day?"

I press my lips together, almost unable to believe I'm telling her. "So . . . that actually already happened."

Her attention cuts to my face as her mouth drops open. "And I didn't even get invited to the wedding?" She holds up a hand. "I kid, but seriously? You . . . I knew you were holding some things back, but this is big. And I'm not just talking about your ring."

"Let's just say . . . it was spur of the moment."

"And the lucky man?"

"You'll meet him eventually."

She plops into the seat across from mine. "I don't even know what to say to you right now."

I wish Lachlan and I had talked about what I could and couldn't say to people, but I go with erring on the side of caution for the moment. "I know, but it's what I wanted."

"You sure? No one held a gun to your head?" she asks, her question completely lacking any semblance of a joking undertone.

I think of the judge and the priest who heard our vows, and all the paperwork we signed. "No. This was of my own free will."

"But you are going to tell me everything eventually. Right?"

"As much as I can."

Temperance inhales, staring at me for long moments until she releases the breath. "Okay. You're the boss. So, what do you want to tackle first?"

When we launch into the list of discussion topics, Temperance proves exactly how much she deserves her new position. I also realize there's no way I'm going to be able to handle everything that needs my attention in only two days.

So, now I have to find a way to get Lachlan back to the negotiation table . . . but luckily, I have an idea.

THIRTY-FOUR

Keira

"I THOUGHT WE AGREED YOU'D BE COMING TO ME, *wife*."

The possessive way Lachlan says the word sends shivers down my spine as he strides out of the elevator and comes toward me.

"Plans change, *husband*. Sit." I gesture to Seven Sinners' most requested table, which is covered with some of the best food New Orleans has to offer, and definitely the best whiskey. "I have more work than I realized, and since that's stopping us from taking a honeymoon . . . I thought you might appreciate a dinner with a view. I can't cook, so this is the best I could do."

One of Lachlan's eyebrows quirks up. "What do mean, you can't cook?"

"You never asked. I hope that's not a deal breaker for you now, because you're stuck with me."

His laughter booms through the empty restaurant.

I decided to keep it closed until tomorrow night, but

begged Odile to come in regardless. I owe her a massive favor now, and from the way she devoured V with her eyes when he followed me into the kitchen, I have a feeling I know what that favor will be.

My sassy Cajun chef won't care that he doesn't speak. She's got enough to say to carry on both sides of the conversation.

"It's fortunate we both employ chefs, or we'd starve," Lachlan says as he pulls out a chair for me, and I sit.

While he rounds the table to take his own seat, I ask, "You can't cook either?"

"Nothing worth eating."

"Good thing I've got you both covered tonight." Odile glides across the floor with an extra swing to her walk as she places my final request on the table. A small cake on a silver platter.

I didn't tell her it's my wedding cake, though, because Lord knows she'd have a million more questions. Somehow, she missed seeing my ring, and I'm thankful for that.

First, I need the man across from me to tell me how the hell I'm going to explain to people that I'm suddenly married, and to whom I can deliver the explanation. I know he said this wouldn't be normal, and I'm not asking for normal, but I do have to tell people *something*. I don't even want to think about telling my family yet.

"Thank you, Odile."

She props a hand on each hip. "Is there anything else I can get for you before I head home?"

"No. This is perfect. I appreciate it."

She sweeps a look over me and then Lachlan. "Bon appétit."

"We both appreciate it, Ms. Bordelon."

I don't know why it comes as a surprise to me that Lachlan knows her last name, but it certainly shocks Odile.

She raises her chin. "I don't need to know nothing except that you're gonna treat her right, sir."

I bite down on my lip, wondering how he'll respond.

"You have my word."

"Then I'll wish you both a good evening and be on my way."

I smile at her as she backs away from the table, her gaze drawn to where V stands near the elevator.

"V, escort Ms. Bordelon down to her car, and then you're free for the evening."

Odile's face lights up at Lachlan's order, and she practically skips toward the silent man.

"You have no idea what you've just unleashed."

Lachlan's gaze comes back to mine. "You don't think she can handle V?"

I glance to where Odile is already chattering at him as they step into the elevator. "I'm not sure he can handle *her*."

Once again, Lachlan's laughter echoes in the room, a sound I want to hear much more often.

When he's finished, he glances at the cake and back at me. "Does she know?"

I shake my head. "I told Temperance the basics, but no one else. I'm not sure what to say to them."

"Whatever is easiest for you. Anything or nothing. Hell, you don't even have to wear the ring if it's going to cause too many questions."

I jerk my hand back and curl the other around it, as though Lachlan might try to take the ring from me. "I'm not taking it off."

A satisfied smile crosses his face. "Good. Because I like seeing it on your finger."

"You don't have one, though. Although, I guess you probably wouldn't wear one, would you?"

"Why wouldn't I?"

"Wouldn't it raise too many questions?"

"No one questions me but you." His smile only widens, and I give him a matching one.

"I'm not going to apologize for that."

"I'll never ask you to."

My smile widens even further as I reach for the whiskey in front of me, lifting it between us.

"To us," I say as he reaches for his own.

"To us," he repeats.

"And to our empire," I add, tearing my gaze away from his to look out at the sun sinking into the New Orleans skyline as the full moon rises.

"*That* I can definitely drink to."

We touch rims before draining the glasses. When mine hits the table, I stare him dead in the eye.

"So, about that butt-plug thing . . . When exactly am I supposed to be ready for that?"

Another laugh reverberates through the restaurant, and I decide Lachlan Mount's laughter is one of my very favorite sounds in the entire world.

"Soon, hellion. Soon."

As we work our way through the feast in front of us, talking about anything and everything that comes to mind, hope for the future grows with every passing minute.

This is arguably the second time I've gotten married on an impulse, although I'd argue the circumstances were entirely different. But this one, I believe, is going to work.

Not just because it has the force of Lachlan Mount behind it, but because we both acknowledge the challenges facing us and are willing to take them on together.

He has offered his help to me in every possible way. His time. His talent. His fortune. Now all I need to do is get him to realize that he's as in love with me as I am with him.

I cut two small pieces of cake and put them on the small extra plates Odile provided, then slide one across the table to Lachlan. "Do you know how this works?"

His brow furrows. "Cake? You eat it."

I smile. "This isn't just *any* cake."

A look of understanding dawns on his features. "Ah, I see. Is this how you're going to talk me into letting you stay and work longer, rather than letting me steal you away to some uninhabited beach?"

"No." I tilt my head. "But how did you know I was planning on that?"

The smile on his face is almost as mesmerizing as his laugh. "Because you love this place, and you won't leave until you're sure everything is running perfectly."

He sees me. Not just the outside I show him, but into the heart of me.

"Are you going to have a problem with that?"

He shakes his head. "I knew exactly who I was getting, and I've been fine with it from the beginning."

"Then you had an advantage over me, because I had no

idea." I pause, trying to figure out exactly how to explain what I want to say, and Lachlan waits silently, almost expectantly. Probably for the worst. But that's not at all what I'm thinking. "You're the most complicated man I've ever met in my entire life."

He opens his mouth to speak, but I continue.

"But not in a bad way, obviously." I nod at the cake in front of me. "I wouldn't have married you if I wasn't already in love with you. And I think I started to fall in love with you when you finally let me see the real you. In Dublin. That's where I finally got to know *Lachlan*, not Mount."

"There isn't one without the other."

"I guess it's a good thing then that I get both." I stand and pick up my cake plate. "So, let's make it official."

He rises, holding his plate. "I thought we did that in front of a priest and a judge."

"You're such a man. It's not official until there's cake and dancing." I meet him at the end of the table.

"Dancing?" he asks, one eyebrow raised.

"Definitely dancing."

He nips my fingers as he snatches the piece of cake away, at the same time feeding me the slice from his plate. Odile's chocolate whiskey cake with Irish cream frosting melts on my tongue.

"Damn, that's good," Lachlan says, and I agree.

"You can have more after the dancing."

He steals the plate from my hand, and they both clatter as he returns them to the table. "There's something that comes before the dancing."

"What's that?"

Lachlan pulls me into his arms. "I get to kiss the bride

for as long as I want."

My cheeks ache from smiling so hard. "I can handle that."

His lips close over mine, and happiness bursts inside me.

THIRTY-FIVE

Mount

IGNORE MY PHONE THE FIRST THREE TIMES IT VIBRATES incessantly in my pocket, but when it starts for the fourth time, Keira giggles and backs away to change the music again.

I pull it out of my pocket, pissed that anyone would dare interrupt what is the closest thing I'll ever have to a wedding reception. Just Keira and me, dancing with candles lit around the restaurant, and the bright light of the moon shining through the thick glass window.

The screen reads *J.*

"What the hell is going on that you can't handle it yourself?"

"Got a tip that the cops are raiding the casino tonight, boss. Thought you'd want to know."

Fuck.

"Tonight? Who the hell don't we have on our payroll? Who'd fucking dare?"

"Apparently, there are more good cops in this city than

either of us realized."

"Shut it down and clear it out."

"Do you want to handle this personally, or do you want me to meet them?"

Keira tips back another glass of whiskey as she hums, scrolling through her playlist, giving me space. I want to stay in this room forever, but this is part of my life. I don't always get the luxury of deciding when the cops are going to raid.

I will, however, make it clear that they are not welcome in my establishment.

"I'm coming."

"You sure? Because—"

"Get it handled. I'll be there."

"Okay, boss. On it."

Keira lowers the empty whiskey glass to the table as her green gaze flashes with worry. "What's wrong? What's going on?"

"Nothing you need to worry about, but I do have to go handle some business." I offer her my hand, and she threads her fingers through mine. "But we'll pick this up again on our honeymoon."

"We're a team now. You can tell me if there's something going on."

I clench my teeth. Her question and tone are so expectant, and my instinctive reaction is to protect her from everything possible. "There will always be things you don't need to know."

"But there are some things that you *can* tell me. If I got a call right now that changed my demeanor as much as that one changed yours, you wouldn't let me leave without an explanation, Lachlan. Besides, no one can force me to testify against you now."

She's right, and I respect her and her desire to know. This isn't something life-or-death that I have to keep to myself, so I decide to share.

"Cops are gonna raid the casino, so I need to be sure a casino isn't there to be raided by the time they arrive."

Her brows wing up to her hairline. "You'd think they'd be happy you just cleaned up the streets for them."

"I'm guessing this is their power play telling me they didn't appreciate my assistance."

"Has this happened before?"

I nod. "Once, when I first took over. They were testing me, and we came to an arrangement. It's been in place a long time. This is just another test, but it won't be an issue."

"Okay. That's all I needed to know. Go do your thing."

I look around the room, not wanting to leave her without V here, but I gave him the damn night off. "Who else is in the building?"

Keira glances down at her watch. "At this time of night? Only Temperance. I told her she wasn't allowed to stay after I left, but she said she wouldn't leave until I do."

"I'll call V and wait for him to come, and then—"

She releases an exasperated sigh. "Go. Handle your business. I'll be fine."

"I'm not leaving you unprotected."

"I've got an arsenal in my office at this point. Anyone who tries to get to me will be dead before they can walk through the doorway. I'm pretty sure Temperance can handle herself too."

Even though she sounds certain, I still don't like the

idea of her being here without V here.

"I'm texting V. Don't even think about leaving the building without him."

Keira presses a kiss to my lips. "Don't worry about me. Go."

I bury my hand in her hair and take the kiss deeper before I pull away. "Later tonight. You, me, no more interruptions."

"Deal."

As I stride toward the elevator, the same uneasy feeling from this morning rides on my shoulder. I send a message to V to get his ass to Seven Sinners ASAP.

THIRTY-SIX

Keira

I HAVEN'T EVEN MADE IT TO MY OFFICE BEFORE MY PHONE starts ringing.

Temperance.

"I'm on my way down," I tell her. "What's going on?"

"Fire alarm at the rackhouse. I just got the call. I had them put me first on the notification list when you were in Dublin. We have to go now. I already called the fire department. They're en route."

Holy fucking hell.

"I'm coming," I yell, then disconnect the call and rush the remaining way to my office.

Temperance is already in the hallway with her purse. "Let's go. I'm driving."

"Good, because I don't have a damned car here." Something I'll be talking to Lachlan about in the event of emergencies just like this.

We run to the parking lot and climb into Temperance's Tahoe.

"We can't lose the rackhouse. That's—" Temperance sounds just as terrified as I do.

"I know we can't. We'll be fucked. This can't be happening right now. It has to be a false alarm."

Temperance hauls ass, the epitome of *drive it like you stole it*, toward the outskirts of town. The rackhouse is a tall, nondescript building that no one would know what was in it unless they paid attention.

When Lachlan basically admitted that he'd had a barrel of the Spirit of New Orleans pilfered from it, I knew I needed to upgrade the security system. But with everything that has happened since, I haven't had time.

Of course this would happen now.

"My dad will disown me if anything happens to that whiskey."

Temperance shoots me a look across the interior of the SUV. "Forget your dad. What the hell would we tell all those distributors we just signed big, fat contracts with?"

We make the rest of the ride in anxious silence, pulling up to the razor-wire fence that surrounds the industrial building. Flames shoot from one of the top-floor windows, but there's not a fire truck in sight.

"Holy fuck!"

Temperance punches in the gate code, and her tires spit gravel as she skids into the parking lot and jams the SUV in park.

"Where is the fire department?" I ask.

"I don't know! I called them. The dispatcher said they'd be here soon."

Not a siren can be heard, and my stomach flips. "Call them again. Right now. I'm going for a fire extinguisher."

She grabs my arm before I can open the car door. "Are you fucking kidding me? You can't go in there."

"This is my legacy. I'm not going to watch it burn to the ground without doing a damned thing to stop it."

I jump out of the car and sprint toward the building, heading around the side entrance.

My phone clutched in my hand, I pull up Lachlan's contact, but before I can tap CALL, something heavy connects with the back of my head.

All I feel is sharp pain before everything goes black.

THIRTY-SEVEN

Mount

THE CASINO FLOOR IS PARTIALLY CLEARED WHEN I arrive, but not completely. It'll be done before the cops get there, though, and I'll be waiting to have a discussion that shouldn't be necessary. By the time they leave, there will be no question that this city still belongs to me.

I text V.

MOUNT: *You have her?*
V: Not yet. On my way.
MOUNT: *Tell me when you have her.*
V: Will do.

I help haul away tables, filling truck after truck that will leave the city in different directions, until sweat drips down my collar.

V hasn't texted me back yet, and it's been almost forty minutes. Something doesn't feel right.

MOUNT: You have her?
V: She's not here. I've been looking. Can't find her.

I've lived my life on gut instinct, and I should have listened to it. Something is totally off.

MOUNT: FIND HER NOW.

My next call is to J. "Did we miss anyone? Anyone at all?" I don't have to specify what I'm talking about.

"No, boss. We got them all. Every single fucking one."

"Are you absolutely certain? Because if you're wrong—"

"I'm not wrong. What the hell is going on?"

"V can't find Keira at the distillery. Something's not right."

"V couldn't find his way out of a paper bag. It's a big building. He's probably lost himself."

J's dismissive tone pisses me right the fuck off, and I don't bother responding. I hang up.

THIRTY-EIGHT

Keira

I WAKE UP, MY HANDS BOUND BEHIND MY BACK. A HORRID stench fills my nostrils.

"Oh God. What is that?"

"Fucking bitch. You just won't die, will you?"

My eyes snap open, focusing on the beam of a flashlight and the blond woman standing just beyond it, her hair almost white in the moonlight. I've never seen her before in my life.

"Who the hell are you?" I choke out the words as the nasty smell threatens to bring up everything I ate tonight.

"I'm the only one who understands him. I'm the one who gets to be with him. I'm his destiny."

"What the fuck are you talking about?" I struggle to sit up, but my hand touches something that crunches and crumbles beneath it.

I take my eyes off her for one second to look down at what else the flashlight beam has illuminated.

"Oh my *God*." I'm lying on top of a pile of bodies.

Skeletons. Decomposing corpses. All wearing women's clothes.

Moonlight sneaks through cracks in the ceiling, revealing that I'm in a mausoleum.

No. No, this is not happening. I'm having a nightmare.

Bile rises in my throat as she raises the barrel of a gun in my direction.

"When you want something done right, you always have to do it yourself."

She pulls the trigger just as I try to push up and scramble back. The bullet punches through my shoulder with a searing, burning stab of pain, its impact stealing my breath as I fall sideways onto something softer.

The flashlight beam bounces as she turns to leave, but before she shuts the door, the light lands on a face inches from mine.

Magnolia's face.

Oh God. No.

"What the fuck did you do, you crazy bitch?" I scream.

"You're the crazy bitch. He was mine first, and he'll always be mine. That was your mistake. You won't make it again. None of you get a second chance," the woman says as the last sliver of light disappears, leaving me shot and bleeding next to my best friend.

"Help!" I scream until my voice grows weak and everything goes black again.

THIRTY-NINE

Mount

"**W**HERE THE FUCK ARE YOU?" I ASK J. "THE COPS haven't shown up. Who the fuck gave that tip? Because if that was bullshit, someone's head will roll."

"He's a reliable source. I'm on my way. Be there in five, boss."

V still can't find Keira. Temperance's car is gone. J is on the way, and I'm losing my fucking mind.

The necklace. Her GPS tracker. Keira still has it on.

I pull up the app and wait for it to load for what seems like a million years.

No signal. I forgot that here on the casino floor, we've blocked all wireless and internet access.

Fuck. Fuck.

I rush out of the casino and through the hallways to my office. Once there, I attempt to get the app to load on my phone and bring up my computer screens at the same time. When I finally get it to load on my desktop, J enters my office.

"This doesn't make any fucking sense," I whisper. The location is one I know, a place I visit at least twice a year. It has to be wrong.

"Did V find her, boss?"

"No. V didn't fucking find her. I just did, and I need you to tell me what the fuck is going on."

I look up at J's face, her pale blond hair tumbling down around her shoulders rather than up in the tight bun she normally wears.

"Calm down, Mikey. It's gonna be fine."

"Don't you fucking call me that. You know better, J."

Seventeen years earlier

My pager vibrated with a number I recognized all too well, followed by the digits *911*.

Fuck, what the hell kind of trouble had Hope gotten herself into now? I knew she struggled. We all fucking struggled because of the shit we'd been through.

The day Hope Jones had walked up the steps to the foster home from hell, I'd known nothing would ever be the same. It was a gut thing.

The first man I'd ever fucking killed was that piece of shit, Jerry, who had his dick out, ready to rape a fourteen-year-old girl. I'd hoped getting her out of that house before he could touch her would put her on a better path, and it did—for a while.

Those years I spent on the streets, there wasn't much

I could do except watch to make sure Hope and Destiny didn't leave their new home bruised or looking the worse for wear. I watched over them both the best I could. When Morello brought me into the organization, he owned my life. Eventually, I gained a little more power, and I used that power to make sure Hope graduated from high school and was able to get custody of Destiny.

I'd paid their bills for years, and not just because Hope hadn't gotten a degree yet. I felt responsible for them. You didn't watch out for two people for this long and just forget about them.

At least, I didn't.

Maybe that was the problem. I should have made Hope take on more responsibility for her own damn life. She'd been trying college for years and still didn't have a diploma to show for it, but I didn't make her get a full-time job instead.

Mostly because I wanted her around for Destiny. Hope might not be the best example, but she was a hell of a lot better than anything I had growing up.

Plus, Destiny was smart as hell, and she had a future that both Hope and I wanted to protect.

I left my office, the same office where I ended Morello's life for touching another girl the way Jerry dared touch Hope, with brass knuckles and a Zippo lighter in one pocket, a switchblade in the other, and twin .45s strapped under my suit coat. I didn't bring a fucking knife to a gun-fight anymore.

Hell, I didn't even have to go to the gunfight anymore. But this wasn't something I was willing to delegate. Hope and Destiny had always been personal.

It only took me ten minutes to get to the house I'd bought for Hope. Inside, dishes shattered and a man yelled.

Destiny was cowering outside under the front steps, rocking back and forth. She was almost eighteen, but curled up and terrified, she reminded me of the five-year-old I first knew.

"What the fuck is going on?" I asked her.

"I don't know. He's . . . he's really pissed. Hope woke him up by accident, and he started going off. She got between us, and I ran. I can't hear her anymore, Mikey. I'm scared." Destiny sniffled back tears. "Why can't I hear her?"

I was already taking the steps two at a time, too focused on the situation to tell her not to fucking call me by that name. Michael Arch died when he was thirteen.

I burst through the front door, my gun drawn and sweeping the room.

I wasn't the only one with a gun in this house, though. A man stood behind the kitchen island, tossing plate after plate onto the floor as a revolver hung from his right hand.

"Stupid fucking bitch. You know better than to make noise when I'm sleeping." He threw another plate.

Destiny was right. I couldn't hear Hope, and I wasn't going to fire a shot until I knew where she was, even though all I wanted to do was put a bullet in that fucker's head for scaring the hell out of Destiny.

"Turn the fuck around, asshole."

He swung drunkenly around, his ancient-looking revolver coming up as he pointed it at me sideways, gangster-style. *Fucking idiot.*

"Who the fuck are you?"

"Where the hell is Hope?"

"None of your fucking business."

He lifted his other hand and cocked the hammer, which was when I noticed something dark dripping from the pistol's grip.

Blood. I'd seen enough in my life to recognize it easily.

"Put that gun down, right the fuck now, or I won't shoot you. I'll fucking skin you alive while you scream for mercy."

"Don't you talk to me like that. You're worse than that mouthy bitch, but I shut her up just fine."

I moved toward him, the scent of sour sweat, body odor, and booze getting stronger with each step.

"What the fuck do you think you're doin'—"

I pulled the trigger on my .45 before he could finish his sentence, and he screamed as the revolver fell from the dangling, mangled appendage that used to be his hand. The gun landed on the floor and discharged. *Fucking hell. That shouldn't be possible.*

"You fuckin' shot me!" He waved around the remains of his hand as blood spurted wildly, and then his gaze dropped to the floor. "And her!"

My heart, the black hunk of coal in my chest, stopped beating for a second.

"What?"

I dashed around the counter and found Hope's prone body on the linoleum, curled up in a defensive position like he'd been kicking the shit out of her. Shattered glass from the plates covered the floor, and blood dripped from little cuts on her arms and legs. But that wasn't all.

Destiny charged into the house, a baseball bat in her hands. A fucking Louisville Slugger. It wasn't the same one

I'd used, but it was still all too similar to my first murder weapon.

"Don't let him hurt her again!" she screamed from the doorway, ready to come to her older sister's defense.

I didn't know if my presence gave her the courage, or if she'd had to do this before. The word *again* slammed into my brain as my gaze locked on the massive hole in Hope's chest, and her blood-soaked hair where it looked like he'd pistol-whipped her. Both wounds oozed puddles around her body. Her chest didn't move.

"You fucked with the wrong women, asshole."

I fired, blowing off most of his other hand, and Destiny sprinted for the kitchen. I caught her around the waist, trying to stop her from seeing what I saw.

Her sister's dead body.

There wasn't a doubt in my mind that Hope was gone.

The only thing I didn't know was who killed her—the piece of shit writhing on the floor next to her, two pulpy stumps at the ends of his arms, or me because I shot the pistol out of his hand.

The possibility twisted my stomach.

I'm so fucking sorry, Hope.

My attention split, I underestimated how flexible Destiny was and she slipped out of my arms.

"No, Desi!" I grabbed her just as her bare foot landed on a shard of glass. I scooped her up into my arms and turned her face against my chest.

"Let me go!"

"No. You don't need to see that."

"But Hope—"

"Hope is dead, Desi. I'm so fucking sorry." My voice

was hoarse with more emotion than it had held in years.

"No!" She screamed as I carried her out of the house, her tears soaking my shirt. The screams turned into heart-breaking sobs. "Please. No. No. No."

Destiny was all but limp when I got to the car. When I sat her down in the front seat, she sprang into action again, clawing me, trying to get back to the house and Hope.

I gripped her skinny shoulders and shook her to get her attention. "You're not going back in there. Understand me?"

"Mikey—"

"Mount," I said, correcting her out of habit because she couldn't seem to forget the past. Well, fuck, neither of us were going to forget today.

"Hope . . ."

I met Destiny's tear-filled gaze. "Pull it together, Desi. Right now. Hope is gone."

"She can't be dead." Destiny's voice was filled with such heartbreak, what was left of my own heart cracked along with it. She sniffled and wrapped both arms around her legs, curling up into a ball in the front seat, rocking back and forth.

"I'm so fucking sorry, but she is. You're not, though, and we're getting you the hell out of here. I'm gonna take care of you, just like I always have, Desi. You understand me?"

Destiny's head bobbed as she rocked. Her tears stopped falling as she bit her lip and nodded. It showed incredible fortitude for a teenager to switch off her emotions so quickly.

"Please don't leave her in there with him," she begged

me. "Please don't."

"Don't worry. I'm not leaving her behind. I'd never leave her behind. Can you be strong for me?"

"Yeah. Yeah. Please, just get her."

"Breathe, Desi."

She nodded again, still rocking, but hauled in a deep breath.

I shut the door and headed first to the shed next to the house. It took me all of thirty seconds to find a can of gasoline. I ran inside and up the stairs, then poured it on every flammable surface except the bedroom quilt. That I tore off the bed before I ran downstairs and carefully wrapped Hope's body in it.

The piece of shit beside her had already lost consciousness. I'd never know what truly happened before I got here, but it didn't matter now.

I grabbed the Zippo in my pocket, then lifted Hope into my arms and headed for the exit. Before it slammed shut behind me, I flipped open the lighter and struck it. When I tossed it onto the living room floor, the gasoline ignited. I strode toward the car, heat from the fire on my back, and Destiny's stricken face staring at me through the window.

Hefting Hope's body higher, I opened the back door and laid her inside across the seat. "Don't you fucking look back there, Desi."

She jerked her gaze forward as I shut Hope inside. I flung open the driver's side, dropped into the seat, and turned the key.

"You're not going to fucking LSU anymore, Desi. You're getting a hell of a lot further out of this town."

Sirens wailed in the distance as I burned rubber on the cracked pavement, leaving the burning house behind.

Destiny sniffled, reining in her grief the same way I shut down mine. "I want to stay with you."

I didn't look at her as I blew through a stop sign. "No. Not an option. Pick any college you want, and you'll get in. But you're not staying here. I want you as far away from me as possible."

We were almost back to the Quarter when Destiny finally spoke again.

"I heard MIT has a really good computer-science program."

I turned to look at her. Resilient as fuck. Another flower growing between the sidewalk cracks. "Then MIT it is."

We never talked about Hope again. Before I shipped Destiny off to MIT, I tried to bring up her sister, but Destiny shut down completely, like a broken toy.

I never told Destiny that I buried Hope in a mausoleum outside of town, and made sure she always had fresh flowers on the anniversary of her death and on her birthday.

I also never told Destiny that I hadn't forgiven myself for what happened that day. For not protecting them better. For not getting there sooner. For not knowing whether I killed Hope.

Instead, I focused on the future, making sure Destiny's was settled. That was all I could do.

FORTY

Keira

Present day

FIGHT THROUGH THE DARKNESS AND OPEN MY EYES. Pain radiates throughout my entire body, and it's a hell of a lot worse than after the car accident.

The only light in the crypt comes from the full moon sneaking through the cracks in the mortar in one upper corner. It's not enough to see the horror of what's around me, but I can smell it.

"Mags?" My voice breaks in a whisper as I steel myself against the pain and reach out to touch her. "Mags, you can't be dead. Please."

Our last words were spoken in anger, and I can't live with that.

If I get to live.

Fearful of what my fingertips will encounter, I skim them along the silk of her kimono until I hit the skin of her neck.

She's still warm.

"Mags!" I scream her name this time, but get no response.

I don't know how long it takes a body to cool after the life has drained from it, but I refuse to believe that's what's happening here.

"You can't be dead, Magnolia Marie. I refuse to believe it."

My left shoulder pulses with each heartbeat, telling me blood is pumping out of my body. I have to stop the bleeding, but first, I need to know if Magnolia is dead.

I find her carotid artery and close my eyes, blocking out my own pain as I pray to God to find a sign of life.

At first, I feel nothing. But then . . . *There it is.* Thready. That's the word they use on those ER shows, right? She's not dead.

"Mags! Wake the fuck up!" I reach out to touch her face, wishing she would answer me, but she doesn't.

I'm in a silent tomb, surrounded by the bodies of who I have to believe are the missing mistresses. Maybe even Richelle LaFleur.

But how?

Lachlan Mount, the man I married, wouldn't kill an innocent woman. But that blond bitch? She sounded as fucking crazy as hell.

Who the hell is she, though?

"Stay with me, Mags," I whisper as I rip off the right sleeve of my blouse to press against my left shoulder. Blood soaks the fabric in seconds.

I'm bleeding out. I don't know how I know it, but I am.

But if I die, Magnolia dies with me. I can't stomach the thought.

I attempt to push myself up and stand, desperate to find us both a way out, but agony rips through my body. Black spots dance across my vision as I collapse into the horrific mess with a crunch and a squish.

No, I have to try again. My reserves of strength drain to empty as pain swamps my senses.

As I start to black out again, one last clear thought streaks through my brain.

Lachlan will burn this city to the ground if anything happens to me.

FORTY-ONE

Mount

KNOW THE LOCATION OF THE GPS COORDINATES WAY too well. And it makes no sense. Or maybe it makes too much sense . . .

It's not possible.

I shove away from my desk, grabbing a pistol from the desk drawer.

"What are you doing?" my second-in-command asks.

"Going to find my wife."

"You married that whore?"

At her words, everything becomes crystal fucking clear.

My gaze snaps to J's face. "Watch your fucking mouth when you talk about her, and tell me what the fuck you did." I level the pistol on her.

J came to me after four years and a double major at MIT, spending her weekends and school breaks undergoing private combat training usually reserved for professional security. Battle-hardened was what she called herself as she demanded a place in my organization, saying New Orleans was her home, and I was her only family.

I told her if I let her stay, no one could ever know who she was. And like everyone else in my organization, she became known by only a letter. The first letter of her last name—Jones.

"How could you marry her!" The shriek bounces off the walls.

"What did you do, J?"

"Call me Destiny, dammit!"

She rocks back and forth on her heels, looking like the broken girl I found hiding under the stoop, but I can't think about that. Right now, my gut is telling me she's behind all of this.

"If you don't tell me what you did with Keira in the next two seconds, I'll kill you where you stand. History be damned."

Betrayal and shock flash across her face before her gaze turns hard. "I did what I had to do."

"If you fucking laid a finger on her, I swear to God—"

"What? You gonna kill me, Mikey? After all this time? She was in the way. They were all in the way, but I took care of them as soon as you were done so we didn't have any loose ends. Then that madam bitch overstepped her place, giving you one that wasn't a whore. At least, at first. She should've known better than to try to trick you. No one does that and lives."

"What did you do to her?" I growl out the words.

"You weren't supposed to love her. You were only supposed to love me. So I buried her like the rest of them!"

My roar fills the office a second before I pull the trigger.

The bullet slams into her hand, and she screams as blood spurts out.

D rushes into the room, his eyes darting from J to me and back.

"Boss?"

"Lock J up. Don't you fucking lose sight of her or I'll kill you both. Z and I are going to find my wife, and you all better pray she's still alive."

FORTY-TWO

Keira

LOSE TRACK OF TIME, WAKING UP AND FIGHTING TO stay conscious. I scream until my voice gives out. I can't find any wounds on Magnolia's body, but I wrap mine around hers. Neither of us is going to make it much longer.

The roar of an engine brings my focus back to the outside world. Outside this tomb where I've been sure I'm going to die.

I scream, pulling Magnolia's head against my chest, and my fingers touch something sharp.

Her hair chopsticks.

I yank one free, gripping it in my right hand. If that bitch is back, she's gonna be the one to die.

My thoughts are jumbled, and my body screams in pain as I try to stand.

Bones crunch beneath me, and I gag at the scent of decomposition. It's something I'll never forget for however long I have left to live.

"Help!" I scream, my voice breaking. I lose my balance

and fall forward, landing face-first on a corpse, and the silver stake flies out of my hand.

The hinges of the door release a metallic screech as the solid wood panel flies open.

My plan is to rise out of the bodies and stab that bitch through the heart, but I've lost my only weapon.

"Hold on. Hold the fuck on. Don't you fucking die on me, Keira!"

It's Lachlan's voice.

Or am I dreaming again?

I can't separate reality from nightmares anymore. At least, until I lift my head and a flashlight beam blinds me.

"Keira!"

"Lachlan?"

He reaches inside and his hand wraps around mine. "Don't you fucking die on me, hellion. Not now. Not ever."

I blink, and his panicked gaze spears me through the heart as mine seems to give out. Black spots obscure his face, and I croak out one final request.

"Mags. Save Mags too."

FORTY-THREE

Mount

FEAR. IT'S NOT A FEELING I'VE HAD IN YEARS, BUT IT grips me like a demon from hell as Keira's eyes roll back in her head and I haul her out of a pile of dead bodies in Hope's mausoleum.

I can't process what I'm seeing right now. It's not fucking possible. J couldn't have done this. *Or could she?*

I rip off my jacket, using it to staunch the flow of Keira's blood.

Mags. Keira said her name as she passed out, and I yell at Z.

"See if the madam is in there. I'm calling nine-one-one."

In thirty years, I've never gone to a hospital or called the police for help. But for Keira, I would do anything.

The operator's voice sounds tinny in my ear, but maybe it's the blood rushing through it that makes things sound strange as I put pressure on the hole in Keira's shoulder.

Needing to stay calm, I compartmentalize. One part of me loses my goddamned mind at the thought of my wife bleeding out in front of me, while the other recites our location down to the fucking GPS coordinates, issuing threats if they don't get here fast enough. When the dispatcher tells me to hang on the line, I hang up and call the cavalry.

V's phone picks up the call, but he doesn't speak.

"I have her, and I'm not going to lose her." I give him the same directions I did the 911 operator.

As I disconnect the call, Z walks out of the tomb holding the madam's limp body in his arms.

"She dead?"

Z lowers her to the ground beside Keira and feels for a pulse. "Almost. But not yet."

"*Fuck*!"

For the first time in my life, I pray for sirens to be louder, come faster, because my entire world is crumbling. Keira's blood looks almost black in the moonlight as it stains the grass, regardless of the pressure I keep on the wound.

"This is not fucking happening! You will live, goddammit! Don't you fucking leave me! I love you!"

FORTY-FOUR

Mount

THOUGHT HELL WAS THE FOSTER CARE SYSTEM OR living on the streets. I was wrong. Hell is a hospital waiting room, not knowing if the only woman you've ever loved will live or die.

I offer everything I have—including my own fucking life—to God, the devil, and any higher power who will listen if they'll just let her *live*.

Why wouldn't you take me? I'm the piece of shit who doesn't deserve to touch someone as good as her.

Maybe there are some souls that are too black for even hell to want.

I hit my knees, and for the first time in over thirty years, wetness slides down my cheeks as I pray.

FORTY-FIVE

Keira

"**W**AKE UP, HONEY. JUST OPEN YOUR EYES FOR ME. Please, Keira." The voice invades my consciousness.

My eyelids are so heavy. I draw in a breath, but a weight sits on my chest. "Uhhh."

"Keira! Honey! Come back to us. Please."

A hand grips mine and squeezes. My vision blurs around the edges as I force my eyes open.

I want to ask, *What happened?* But it comes out more like "*Whaaarrrppp?*"

"You're okay. You're going to be fine, Keira. Just fine."

My throat hurts. My shoulder hurts. My head hurts. *Everything hurts.* I feel like I never want to move again.

I swear I've felt like this before.

White walls. Antiseptic. Beeping.

Am I dreaming?

A voice in my head yells at me to wake the hell up, and I blink twice before my sight clears.

But the face in front of mine isn't the one I expected to see.

I jerk up in the hospital bed, my head swiveling from side to side. There's no empty bed beside mine this time.

I groan, trying to force another sound from my throat, but it comes out as a scratchy moan.

Where is he? That's the first thought that enters my brain. *Where is Lachlan?*

But it's not the question that leaves my lips.

"Mom?"

"Thank God. Don't you ever scare us like that again." Her green eyes, a shade darker than my own, fill with tears, and her face looks years older than it did in the last picture I saw of her.

"Sweet Jesus. Thank you, Lord." My dad's deep voice overpowers hers as he steps into my field of vision.

"Dad?" It doesn't make sense. *How did my parents get here? And where is Lachlan?* "How—"

"Shhh, honey. Don't talk. They had you under for hours in surgery. They said your throat would hurt from the breathing tube. Jesus Christ, when we got the call from the alarm company and then you didn't answer, and then Millie called a few hours later saying you'd come in alone in an ambulance—" *Alone?* My mom's voice breaks. "We broke every law to get here as fast as we could. She didn't know if you were going to make it."

Millie? My brain is slow to start chugging along as I search the room again, looking beyond them for the one face I need to see but know I won't find.

Millie. My mom's cousin, and an ER nurse. That explains how my parents found out . . . but *alone*?

"What happened?" I ask again, my brain fuzzy from whatever drugs they've pumped through me. "Where—"

"You were shot," my dad says. "EMTs and the ambulance that brought you in are missing. What the fuck happened to you, girl?" My dad's tone is layered with anger and fear, and more emotion that I've heard from him in a long time.

When I swallow and my lips crack, my mom springs into action.

"Water. You need water." She has the bendy straw to my mouth before I can reply.

I take a sip, and it trickles down my throat with cool relief. "Shot?"

"Shhh, honey. It's okay. You don't need to worry right now. Just . . . rest. We're just so happy to see your pretty eyes. Let me call for the nurse."

"I need to know who the hell hurt my little girl, so I can get my shotgun and shovel and take care of business." My dad's gruff words pull me further out of the haze.

"I don't know," I murmur, and close my eyes. They're still so freaking heavy.

"Anything. Name. Place. Hair color. I'll hunt them down myself."

"Shhh, David. Stop it."

"Don't tell me to stop it, Kath. Someone shot my little girl."

I keep my eyes closed while my parents argue quietly. My lungs draw in and release one shallow breath at a time, and I focus on that because nothing else makes sense.

My memory is so fuzzy. Worse than the morning I woke up in Dublin.

Dublin.

"Dance with me, Lachlan. Dance with me in Dublin."

"Where is he?" My croaking question rivals a bullfrog in the swamp.

"Who?" my dad demands. "The man who did this?"

I try to shake my head, but moving it makes me too dizzy. *Is that a bandage wrapped around it?*

I attempt to lift my arm to touch it, but it's so heavy. No, it's strapped down.

"What happened?" I ask again as I tilt my gaze downward to see a sling around my shoulder.

"That's what we're asking you."

Bodies. Magnolia. Oh my God.

"Mags?"

"Did she have something to do with this?" My mom's voice rises an octave. "Is she involved?"

I'm saved from having to answer any more questions when the door opens and several people enter.

"Ms. Kilgore, so happy to see you awake. How are you feeling?" a blond woman asks, and I tense.

Blond. My breathing picks up.

"Who are you?" My words come out on huffs of breath.

"She's the doctor, honey. She's been here all along. And here's Millie. She's been hanging around all night, waiting with us."

I stare at the blond woman, my body's fight-or-flight response poised for flight. *Is that her?* The fractured pieces of my memory are still cracked and broken, so I don't know. My hands curl into claws, but I have no weapon. Nothing to keep me safe.

She's the doctor. That's what my mom said, but I can't

trust anyone. Not now. *Where is Lachlan?*

I look beyond the blonde, hoping to find his dark gaze on me, but all I see is a plump brunette who always has a ready smile on her face.

"Good to see you awake, Keira," Millie says.

"Can you tell us how you're feeling?" the doctor asks me again.

"Tired. Sore." I keep my answers short. Not only do I not trust her, but my brain feels broken.

"I imagine. You sustained a gunshot wound in addition to head trauma. Can you remember what happened?"

I shake my head, but it's a bad idea. Dizziness assails me, and I'm reminded of the last time I woke up in a hospital-like setting.

"I don't remember anything," I tell her. I don't even have to try to make it sound convincing. My voice is wrecked.

"Does she have amnesia?" my mom blurts out.

"It's possible that she could have some memory loss due to the head injury."

I want to tell my mom I don't have amnesia. I just can't grasp all the pieces floating through my mind, because without the one man who should be in this room, nothing makes sense. My left hand curls into a weak fist against my chest, and I still, my gaze darting down.

My ring is gone. I lift my right hand to my throat. *My necklace is gone too.*

The doctor speaks to my parents, but I tune it all out as a terrifying question slams into my brain.

Did I imagine all of it? Is that why he's not here? Is Lachlan Mount a figment of my imagination?

No. That's not possible. He's real. What we have is real.

Isn't it? *He's not a ghost. He's real. Right?*

I look around the room, blood rushing in my ears, drowning out everything but my own thoughts.

"What happened?" I force the question out, and everyone around me goes quiet.

"That's what we'd really like to figure out, Keira," the doctor says. "Don't push yourself. Just rest. Some of your memories may come back if you let your brain rest."

"Are you sure?" Again, another panicked question from my mom, but I want to demand answers too.

The doctor pauses. "It's possible she may not remember everything. We'll just have to wait and see."

"Wait and see? Someone shot my little girl!"

"David!" Mom snaps, and Dad quiets.

Then everyone fusses over me, checking my heart and my breathing, taking my blood . . . and I let my eyes drift closed again.

The next time I wake up, my mom is still there but my dad is gone. I'm less fuzzy this time but still totally confused, because the man I want to see in my room is missing.

I can't ask about him. My mom doesn't know Lachlan Mount exists.

But I do. He is real. I know that. *Where is he, then?*

"Honey, drink some more water." Again, Mom lifts the bendy straw to my lips and I sip. "Your dad is going out of his mind."

"I'm sorry."

"Shhh. This isn't your fault. You didn't ask to be shot.

I'm sure of that. But the police have been waiting, and they have a lot of questions that we don't have any answers to, except . . ."

"What?" I ask, my gaze locking on hers.

"The fire at the rackhouse. They found your assistant."

"Temperance! Is she okay?"

How the hell could I have forgotten about her?

"Hush. Don't get worked up. She's fine. She got clubbed over the head. The fire department found her unconscious just inside the building when they busted down the door."

"Oh my God." My heart slams into my chest when I think of what could have happened to her. "She's okay, though?" Tears burn behind my eyes. This is all because of me. Temperance could have died, and it would all be my fault.

"She's fine. Smoke inhalation. They were lucky they got to her in time. They kept her overnight for observation for her head, but released her the next morning. She just went to go to the bathroom. She's been keeping vigil with us here ever since."

The next morning? *How much time have I missed?*

"What day is it?"

"You've been sleeping on and off for two days, honey."

"Two days?"

My mom nods. "She's been at your bedside with your dad and me. She's a good friend to you."

Friend. The word triggers another piece of my broken memory to snap into place.

"Magnolia." Her name bursts from my lips. "Is she . . . Is she . . ." I can't voice the last word, but I remember her smooth skin and thready pulse under my fingertips.

My mom's features tense and her lips wobble. "She's in a coma, Keira. They don't know if she's gonna make it."

I squeeze my eyes shut. "No. No. She can't— We . . . I need to talk to her. She can't—"

"Shhh. It's okay. We're praying for her too. The doctors are taking care of her. I've checked in on her myself. I knew you'd want me to."

I can't fathom my last words to my best friend being those of anger, regardless of what she did. Conflicting emotions wring tears from my eyes, and I want to beg for someone to tell me where Lachlan is, but I can't.

My dad reenters the room with Temperance behind him. Two police officers trail after them.

"Keira!" Temperance rushes around Dad to reach me first. "Oh, thank God. You're awake."

"I'm so sorry," I tell her.

"For what? This isn't your fault."

That's where she's wrong. Even with my battered body and nearly broken brain, I know that this is one hundred percent my fault. Nothing would have happened to Temperance if not for me.

"Ms. Kilgore, do you think you might be able to answer a few questions for us?"

"Not right now, gentlemen." A nurse sweeps in and comes toward me, ready to poke and prod and do whatever it is they've been doing for the last couple of days. "You need to let her rest."

"With all due respect, ma'am, we need some answers so we can carry on our investigation."

Temperance turns toward them. "You don't think working with the fire department to figure out who started the fire at the rackhouse is enough to keep you busy? Because we sure as hell don't have any answers to that one yet. Or who clubbed me over the head? You could maybe try to figure that one out."

"Ma'am, it's not our fault your security cameras malfunctioned completely."

"What? How?" I ask.

"Sorry, ma'am. We don't know," the officer says. "It's been ruled as arson, but they're still working on the motive."

"Then you better work on that, because I already told you, we didn't do it." Temperance's tone is bullwhip sharp. "We need every freaking barrel to fill the orders we have. So, if you're looking for insurance money as a motive, you need to go back to detective school."

"We weren't implying—"

"Of course you weren't," my dad says, interrupting him. "Because no Kilgore or Seven Sinners employee would ever let something happen to that whiskey. It's our blood. Our heritage. Our legacy." My dad gives Temperance an approving nod like they're a team.

Shafts of guilt stab into me because I know I caused this. Neither of them have a clue. "I'm sorry, Dad—"

He snaps around to look at me. "This isn't your fault. Whoever did this is going to pay. We'll make them pay."

I blink as tears burn my eyes once more. The one man who could answer every single one of these questions is gone.

Was the blonde behind all of it? I remember bits and pieces of her. *His destiny.* Who was she, though?

"Mr. Kilgore, Ms. Ransom, we're not trying to suggest that you had something to do with this. We're just looking for answers the same way you are."

"I don't remember." Everyone looks at me as the lie leaves my lips. "I don't remember anything. I'm sorry. I wish I could help."

My insides are shredding—old loyalties versus new. Regardless of what happened and why, telling the cops isn't going to help. Justice is delivered differently now. *At least, it will be if he ever comes back.*

I squeeze my eyes shut as the same question bounces through my brain like a pinball. *Where is he?*

"I'll leave my card in case you remember anything," the cop says, and I can't read his tone.

Am I a bad liar? Can he tell?

"We'll be sure to call, but in the meantime, do your damned jobs."

My dad's farewell sends the officers out of the room as I attempt to piece together the rest of what happened. I open my eyes, fixing my gaze on Temperance. I need to talk to her alone, but I don't think my mom is going to let that happen.

"Are you okay?" I ask her.

My COO nods. "I'm fine. I come from strong stock. It would take more than a whack to the head to end me."

"Your brother . . ."

Her eyes narrow meaningfully. "He's looking into things."

Is that what Lachlan is doing too? Is that why he's not here?

Temperance glances down at my naked left hand and then meets my gaze. "Anyone else you want me to call?"

"Do you have my phone?" Another memory slips into

place. I was going to call Lachlan when everything went dark.

"No. Do you remember where you lost it?"

The implications of not having a phone have never been quite so dire. Without my phone, I can't contact my husband. I don't know his number.

"The rackhouse. I had it there," I tell her, panic rising.

"No one said they found it, but I can call anyone you want."

I bite my lip. "I . . . I appreciate the offer. But I really need my phone."

Temperance nods, understanding dawning on her features. "I'll ask the firefighters. Maybe they found it and kept it as evidence, and forgot to mention it."

"Thank you."

"What else can I do?"

"You can leave her alone to rest," my dad says, his voice gruff now that he's chased away two cops. Apparently, his respect for Temperance has worn off quickly.

"Dad, stop. Temperance is my COO. She's amazing. Be nice."

"COO?" His head jerks toward her. "Thought you were a secretary."

"Stop," I say, my voice weakening. "I can't handle this right now."

"David, I need more coffee," my mom says.

"But I just got you—"

"More. Now."

My dad grumbles and turns to leave.

Mom gives me an apologetic look. "Sorry, honey. He's been worked up."

Temperance reaches down and threads her fingers through mine. "Do you want me here, or do you want me to hold down the fort?"

"You should be home, resting."

"Boss, you know me better than that. Besides, I just got knocked on the head. No one put a hole in me. I'm fine."

"I'm not asking you to work. No way."

She smiles. "You don't have to. I'd do it anyway. If you need *anything* at all, call me."

As she releases my fingers, I want to beg her to find Lachlan and bring him to me, but I never even told her about him in precise terms. The only person in my world who knows about him is Magnolia, and she's somewhere in this hospital, in a coma. Because of that crazy blond bitch.

Who was she? Is that why he's gone? Did she hurt him? The thought crushes me, sending me mentally stumbling backward. *Is he dead?*

No. No. No.

I refuse to believe that.

Lachlan Mount is superhuman. Not even a bullet could stop him. It didn't before.

Then why isn't he here? I'm torn between anger and desperation, willing to bargain away my soul just to see his face and make sure he's okay.

He wouldn't leave me. He *wouldn't*.

I'm tiring again, but I have to ask my mom one very important question.

"Have I had any other visitors, Mom?" When she nods, my heart lifts. "Who?"

"Pretty much everyone we know in this town has stopped by. Your dad has kept them all in the hall, but it's been quite the parade."

"Anyone . . . anyone you didn't know?"

Her brow creases. "What do you mean, honey?"

I want to ask her so badly, but I can't. Instead, I take the coward's way out and close my eyes to feign sleep as my heart cracks again.

Where is he?

FORTY-SIX

Keira

"**D**ance with me, Lachlan. Dance with me in Dublin."

His face, normally so stern, has changed tonight. He has changed tonight. When he takes my hand and pulls me into the crowd of dancing Irish men and women, a smile turns his mouth into the most beautiful thing I've ever seen.

"You're beautiful," I tell him. I'm drunk and I don't care.

"Men aren't beautiful."

"Lies. All lies. Because you are."

He spins me as we pretend we know this Irish jig, and brings me back against his hard body. "We'll agree to disagree."

"Fine. But I'm still right."

His smile brightens the entire room. I swear it could light a pitch-black sky. He leans in, his lips brushing against my ear. "Not right, but priceless all the same."

"Pssh. We both know my price. You found it." The answer

flies from my lips without thought, my filter gone, thanks to the booze.

He jerks back, staring down at me, all humor gone from his face. "Don't you say that. Because that is pure bullshit. I couldn't buy you with every penny I have."

"But—"

"But nothing. Whatever you're thinking, I promise, you're wrong."

I'm thinking that I'm in big trouble because my heart is tumbling out of my control as the man who once terrified me now stares at me with warmth and admiration in his gaze.

"Careful, Lachlan. You wouldn't want to get attached to me."

His lips lower, stopping a breath from mine. "Too late."

I jerk awake, expecting to feel a solid man against me, but he's not there.

"Where is he?"

"Ms. Kilgore, are you okay?" The nurse holding my chart tucks it away and comes toward the bed. She's blond.

Instantly I tense. "I'm . . . I'm . . ." I trail off because I have no freaking clue what I am anymore. But *okay* is not it.

"Is the pain getting worse?"

"I'm fine."

"You don't sound fine." She heads for the IV drip, but I don't trust her. I don't trust *anyone* I've seen in this room except Temperance and my parents.

Where the hell are you, Lachlan? I need you.

"Mom? Tell her I'm okay. I don't need more drugs. I

can stay awake." My voice sounds weak, but she's the only defense I have against this unidentified blond woman.

My mom jerks awake. "What? What's going on?"

"I'm just going to adjust her meds, then take her down for a test."

"A test?" My mom sits up straighter in the reclining chair on my right. "What kind of test? What's wrong?"

The nurse glances at my mom, and I look around for a weapon. Just in case. The tray from whatever meal I didn't eat is still on the table beside the bed.

As the blonde explains about some kind of neuro test, I reach for the butter knife with my free hand and tuck it beneath the sheet. It's not much, but it's better than nothing.

The metal bites into my palm, and I remember holding on to Magnolia's silver chopstick I'd had made for her. I was going to stab that blond bitch if she came back. I just can't remember her face.

"Everything's fine, Mrs. Kilgore. I promise this is routine. I'll have her back here in no time." The nurse adjusts whatever they're pumping into me from the pole attached to the bed, and releases the brake.

"I'll come with."

My mom rises from the chair, and I wonder if her protective instincts are flaring for the same reason as mine. If this is really the crazy bitch, I don't want my mom anywhere near her. Especially not if I have to stab her with a butter knife.

"We'll be right back. There's no point in you trudging through the halls to wait outside anyway." As my mom wrestles with this decision, the nurse says, "I swear. She's going to be fine."

The nurse's placating tone rubs me the wrong way, and I prepare to do battle. I keep quiet, not wanting to give my mom a reason to come along.

When she finally nods and lowers herself back into the chair, her eyelids droop almost instantly.

"Mom, it'll be okay. I'll be right back. You should sleep." I don't believe what I'm saying, but I tell her anyway.

"Love you, honey."

"Love you too, Mom."

She's already snoring as the nurse wheels me out of sight.

⌒

The hallways of the hospital are quiet, which puts me even more on edge.

"Where are we going?"

"Just another quick check of your head. You took a hard hit."

I almost ask her if she did it, but then I'd lose the element of surprise if it's really her.

My paranoia ratchets up the farther we get away from my room and my mom. Finally, I can't stand it anymore. With the butter knife clutched in my hand, I turn my head, ignoring the pounding pain.

"Who are you, and where the hell are you taking me?"

She steps forward to punch a round silver disk that activates the double doors, and they swing wide.

"No need to panic, Keira. I promise, everything's going to be fine." She turns me toward an open doorway, and there's nothing but darkness beyond it.

"If you try to fucking touch me, I swear to God, I will—"

She raises a hand in a defensive gesture. "No need to threaten. I'm not going to hurt you. I don't have a death wish. I'll give you two a few minutes alone." She pushes me into the dark room and steps back.

You two?

My eyes acclimate to the darkness as her shoes squeak in retreat on the tile floor, and I find his face in the shadows.

FORTY-SEVEN

Mount

SOMETHING METALLIC BOUNCES OFF THE TILE AS Keira bursts into tears.

Fucking Christ, her tears kill me.

"Where have you been?" she asks through a sob as I drop to my knees beside her bed.

Rivers spill down her cheeks, so many that my thumbs can't catch the droplets fast enough. She jerks her face out of my hands as her lungs heave.

I've been dying for more than the glimpses I've gotten of her for days. I could only see her as they wheeled her in and out of her room for tests, and then I'd lose her again when she was pushed into a room. I cursed the hospital for only having security cameras in the halls.

"I've been watching. You've been protected. You're safe. I swear it."

"But where the hell have you been?"

Guilt claws at my chest at the sound of her ravaged voice. I've brought this proud, strong woman to her breaking point. All of this is my fault.

"I couldn't be there. Your mom and dad came before you were out of surgery, so I had to stand down. Pretend it wasn't killing me to wait and find out if you were going to pull through."

"But—"

"When they called your family upstairs, I couldn't go. I couldn't explain who the hell I am to any of them. Who the hell I am to you. That I'm part of your fucking family too." Reliving those moments of helplessness guts me just as badly the second time.

"So, you left me? Alone? For days? Wondering whether that crazy fucking blond bitch killed you too?"

I know exactly which crazy fucking blond bitch she's referring to. "You haven't been alone. Not for a fucking second, Keira. If you had, I would've been in there."

"How is it possible that you—Lachlan Mount—with all your unlimited power, couldn't manage to get me a single sign that you were okay?"

I blink as it finally occurs to me why she's so upset. She's spent this whole time worrying about me too. "I didn't know you needed a sign."

"I've been losing my mind, wondering if you were alive! Wondering if I was crazy. Wondering if anything was real."

"Keira—"

Her tears fall faster. "Nothing makes sense anymore. I don't understand what happened. You have to tell me something. Who was she? And Mags—she tried to kill her too. All those women—"

I cut her off with the press of my fingers to her lips. As much as I want to tell her everything right now, I can't.

"Not here. Not now, Keira. Not yet."

"When? I need to know."

I cup her face, trying once more to catch her tears on my thumbs. "No more tears, hellion. The only thing you need to focus on is getting well. Letting them take care of you."

"No! I need answers, and I need my freaking husband."

"Keira. I can't—"

"Don't tell me there's anything you can't do, Lachlan. Because I won't believe you."

Her conviction rings true, and I wish I deserved it. I don't deserve that kind of faith from anyone. Especially not now.

"That's where you're wrong. If I could do anything, I'd rewind the clock and undo all of this."

FORTY-EIGHT

Keira

HIS WORDS SLAM INTO ME HARDER THAN THE BULLET in my shoulder, and my stomach twists. "All of it? You . . ." I blink, barely able to see through my tears.

His face creases with pain that mirrors my own as the door opens and the nurse returns.

"Do you want me to leave?" she asks, picking up on the tense silence in the room.

"No. Take her back," Lachlan says. "I'm sure her family is worrying every second she's out of their sight."

I open my mouth to say something. *Anything.* But he's not Lachlan anymore. He's Mount.

My lips slam shut, but then I decide *fuck it.* If this is the last time I ever get to see him, I'm going to tell him exactly what I think and feel.

"I'm not done here. *We're* not done here."

He meets my gaze. "I decide when we're done."

My mouth drops open as words so similar to those he spoke that night in his dining room—the first night I left claw marks on his back—fall from his lips.

I turn my head and look over my shoulder at the nurse. My body twinges, pain fighting through the drugs. "Get out."

"Ms. Kilgore—"

"Get. The. Fuck. Out."

The nurse shuffles back and the door closes once more.

I turn and look at my husband. "We are not over. Do you understand me? I took *vows*, and I meant every single word of them."

His face shifts from the hard mask to twisted confusion. "Are you trying to say I didn't?"

"You want to undo all of this? End it?"

He jams a hand into his hair as he stares down at me, looking completely destroyed.

"Jesus fucking Christ, Keira. That's not what I meant but, fuck, it should be. If I had a single shred of decency in my soul, I would take everything back, all the way to the first time I touched you." He sounds like he's forcing the words from his throat. "But even if I had that power, I wouldn't take any of it back. Not a single goddamned second. If that makes me the most selfish motherfucker on this planet, then so be it."

"Then what the hell did you mean?" My tears fall harder now. Partly because nothing makes sense right now, but most of all, because I can't stand to see that tortured expression on his face.

"That I would turn back time to save you even a single moment of pain. Take us back to when we were eating cake and dancing. To before you almost fucking died because of me."

Guilt underpins every single word, and I hate it. This isn't his fault. I refuse to let him shoulder this burden.

"You didn't pull that trigger. *She* did."

"But I should've stopped it. I should've known."

I reach out to touch his arm, drawing strength from him, desperate to take his pain like he wants to take mine. "I know you're superhuman, but even you can't know everything."

The muscles in his jaw tense as he leans down to cup my cheek. "I said I'd keep you safe, and I didn't. That's something I'll have to live with for the rest of my life."

I turn my face into his hand and press a kiss to his palm. "As long as you live with me for the rest of your life, we'll deal with it together."

"Keira—" My name sounds like a prayer torn from his lips.

"I just need to know one thing."

"What?" he asks, cupping my face like he never wants to let it go.

"Am I safe now?"

He nods. "Yes. Completely. I've taken care of everything."

I want to ask a dozen more questions, but like he said—not now. So I settle for the most important one.

"And what happens when they discharge me?"

Lachlan's eyes narrow, his gaze intensifying. "You come home to me. Where you belong."

FORTY-NINE

Keira

MY DISCHARGE PAPERS HAVE BEEN SIGNED. AFTER seven full days in the hospital, I should be rushing out the door, but I'm not.

"Honey, are you sure?" Mom squeezes my shoulder as my wheelchair halts at the door of a private room. A private room I'm willing to bet anything is being paid for by my husband.

"I know you never liked Mags, but—"

Her grip stiffens. "It wasn't that I didn't like her, honey. It was that I didn't want to take a chance that you'd be pulled down her path."

I swallow at her words. *How can I ever tell my mother that I'm standing at the end of a path that is infinitely more dangerous than the one Magnolia has taken?* I'm the queen of a sinful empire, and I plan to spend the rest of my life beside its king.

I especially can't tell her that Magnolia is totally responsible for putting me in that position, and that there's nowhere else I'd rather be.

With the hand that's not strapped to my side in a sling, I reach up and cover hers before looking up at her. "I love you, Mom. Thank you for everything."

"I love you too, honey."

"Now, I need a few minutes alone with Mags. I . . . I have a few things I have to say to her, and I need some space."

She releases my shoulder and steps away. "Okay. I'll be right outside, and Dad is getting everything else in order."

The aide wheels me into the room and parks my chair beside Magnolia's bed, then retreats, shutting the door behind her.

Magnolia's dark hair is wrapped in gauze that covers her entire head. No one would tell me anything about her condition except that she's being monitored and provided the best possible care. She hasn't woken up, and they don't know if she ever will.

I extend my free hand and clutch her limp one. "Magnolia Marie Maison, this is so like you." I sniffle back tears. "Gotta cause all the drama to get the attention and leave the rest of us in suspense, wondering what's going on."

The beeping of the monitors is the only response to my poor attempt at humor.

I squeeze her fingers. "Mags, please. You have to wake up. You're a fighter. You're the toughest woman I know, and you will not let this beat you. Do you understand me? I refuse to let you give up."

The beeping of the monitor stays steady, no indication at all that she hears a single word. But I know there's research out there about people in comas being able to hear what's said around them while they're unconscious. I'm hoping like hell my best friend can hear me now, because if I don't hold on to that belief, I'll end up sobbing at her bedside.

That might happen anyway, though.

I lift Magnolia's hand to my cheek. "Listen to me, woman. You are not leaving the world like this. You don't go quietly. They'll have to tear you off this earth kicking and screaming. Do you hear me? *That's* who you are. Don't you dare let me down. I need you to wake up. I have things to say to you, and I need to know that you can hear them."

The answering silence triggers another torrent of tears.

"I know you did what you thought was right for me. That you *always* do what you think is right for me. I don't care about your other motives, because you gave me a gift I can never repay. I should've thanked you when I had the chance."

Her pulse beats through her wrist and her chest rises and falls, but that's it.

"Mags, how are you going to tell me *I told you so* if you don't freaking wake up so I can tell you this when you're not unconscious?"

I drop my head, tears rolling down her palm now.

"I forgive you. I love you. Please, come back to me. The world would be a darker place without you in it. *My world* would be darker, and I know you don't want that."

I wait for long, silent moments, but she still doesn't wake.

What did I really think was going to happen? That it would be like Sleeping Beauty and somehow my forgiveness would wake my best friend like the prince's kiss? Obviously not.

"I love you, Mags." I press a kiss into her palm and lower her hand to her side. "Come back to us. I promise you'll get all of those sister-of-the-queen benefits."

When we reach the exit, Mom is chattering about the awesome place she and my dad rented for the next few weeks, and how much I'm going to love it. Their rental car idles at the curb. My dad hops out as soon as he sees us, and reaches the sidewalk as another car pulls up behind him.

A black Mercedes-Maybach with blacked-out windows. I don't need to see inside it, though, to know exactly who's driving.

"Would you be more comfortable in the backseat or the front, honey?" Mom keeps talking, debating the question with my dad, not waiting for a response from me.

Which is good, because my attention is on the black car.

The driver's door opens and V steps out. He glances at my parents, but they're totally oblivious. When his attention returns to me, I nod, and we have a wordless conversation.

Yes, I'm ready to go home. Take me to him.

V returns my nod and comes toward me. As I rise from the wheelchair on unsteady legs, V is by my side in an instant.

My mom whips around, she and my dad finally realizing someone else has arrived. "Honey! What are you doing? Who is that man?"

V leads me toward the back door and opens it for me, but before I can get inside, my dad charges toward us. If he had a gun, I'm pretty sure the barrel would be pressing against V's head right now.

"I don't know what the hell you think you're doing, but you get your goddamned hands off my daughter."

"Honey? What's going on? Do you need me to get security?" Fear resonates in my mom's voice, just as strong as my dad's threat hanging in the air.

I can't blame them. They got a call in the middle of the night and found me hanging on to life by a thread. And yet I still can't tell them the truth.

"Mom, Dad, this is my ride. My driver. I promise he won't let anything happen to me. He'll keep me safer than you ever knew was possible."

My dad's gaze narrows on V. "Where the hell was he when you took a bullet, if he's so good at keeping you safe?"

My instinct is to plead with my dad not to argue with me right now, but instead, I straighten my spine as much as is possible with my healing injuries and face him.

"There are things I can't tell you right now, Dad, but I will when I can."

"I don't like this. I don't like this at all." My mom's fingers tangle together in front of her as she frets. "Honey, please, just come with us. Don't get in that car."

V clears his throat. "I'll protect her with my life. I swear it to you." His deep voice sounds rusty from disuse.

Silently, I freak out. *You can freaking talk, V? Are you kidding me?*

My eyebrows climb toward my hairline, but I hold back the questions begging to fall from my lips.

"Who are you? Who do you work for? Have I seen you before?" My dad's jaw tenses, his hands clenched into fists.

V goes silent again, giving me the odd thought that

hearing his voice is equivalent to spotting an albino leopard in the wild. Once in a lifetime.

I meet both of my parents' panicked stares one at a time. "Dad, stand down. Mom, I love you both. I promise I'm fine. I'm going to be safe. I'll be in touch very soon."

"Keira—"

My name is gruff on my dad's lips, and I interrupt him before he can launch into whatever lecture or scolding is coming.

"I'll see you at the distillery tomorrow morning, Dad. I'd really like to have your expertise while I sort out what the hell our next steps are. Seven Sinners was about to step up to the next level, and I refuse to back down."

My dad's head jerks back. "Tomorrow morning? You swear?"

I nod. "Yes. I'll be there. Maybe you should take Mom out to dinner tonight. She has to be missing real crawfish étouffée something fierce."

My father studies me and then V. "I'll expect some answers soon."

I smile, feeling ridiculously regal, even in my sling. "You'll get them when I'm ready. I'll see you both tomorrow."

V helps me into the back of the Maybach, and I'm thankful for the ridiculously comfortable interior. My parents stand motionless beside their car as V climbs into the driver's seat and pulls the car away from the curb.

"So, when were you going to tell me you could actually talk? Don't think I'm going to let this go."

He glances up into the rearview mirror with a grunt. I laugh, the first happy sound to leave my lips in over a week.

I'm going home.

FIFTY

Mount

MAY AS WELL CHANGE MY NAME TO KEIRA, BECAUSE ALL I've done for the last ten minutes is pace the living room of our suite. I tried to work, but my concentration was blown knowing she's on her way home.

Home.

I've never called these rooms by that name, but with her here, everything shifted.

The lock on the outer door disengages and she steps through the threshold, her wild red hair pulled up in a messy bun on top of her head, tendrils hanging loose around her face. V nods at me from behind her and closes the door as soon as she's all the way inside.

My wife.

My lover.

My love.

"He talks!" Keira blurts out.

I blink at her, because it's not what I was expecting her to say first. "What?"

"V! He talked! To my parents. My dad was ready to call security, but V . . . he talked."

A smile tugs at my lips, something only she could make happen in this moment. "He's always been able to talk, hellion. He just chooses not to."

She pinches the fingers of one hand together beside her temple and spreads them wide as she jerks them away. "Mind. Blown."

Laughter rumbles up from my chest, booming through the room. *Only this woman . . .*

I cross the room and carefully wrap my arms around her. "I fucking missed you."

"Good, because it wasn't a picnic without you around either. One clandestine meeting in the depths of the hospital wasn't nearly enough. Let's not do that again, okay?"

I lower my chin to her hair. "Deal."

She pulls her head away from my chest and looks up at me. "Would you kiss me? Please?"

"You're still healing . . ."

Her green gaze pleads with mine. All the humor that followed her through the door has vanished. "I know. But when I woke up in that hospital bed without you there and no ring and no necklace, I thought for a minute . . . with my busted brain . . . I thought maybe none of this was—" Her voice breaks.

"Hellion, stop."

Keira shakes her head. "No. I have to get this out. It matters."

I curve my palm around her cheek and catch a tear that tips over her lid. "Then tell me."

"When I thought there was a chance that I'd made this

all up in my head and that you weren't real . . . it was devastating. I never want to feel like that again. Ever."

My arms tighten around her. "This is as real as it gets. You and me. We're in this for life."

"Promise?"

I release her and dig into my pocket with my right hand, pulling out the ring I had retrieved from her personal belongings.

"This ring doesn't come off your finger again," I tell her as I slip it back on where it belongs.

Her eyes light up at the sight of it before meeting mine and going hard. "They'll have to pry it off my cold, dead hand."

"Don't you fucking say that. I almost broke in that hospital waiting room, thinking I lost you. And I don't ever want to feel that way again either."

She swallows, threatening tears turning her green eyes shiny again as she leans into me. "Kiss me, and we have a deal."

The pain of that memory washes away with the touch of her lips on mine.

FIFTY-ONE

Keira

"**H**E DOES NOT GET TO FORBID ME FROM GOING TO work. I promised my dad I would be there this morning. You heard me. If you think for a second that my dad's not going to call the cops if I don't show up, you're nuts."

V grunts, his fingers flying across his phone as he's returned to his mute state. My phone buzzes with a text, which is a really inconvenient and unsatisfying way to argue.

V: Boss said you stay here.

"Then he's going to have to tell me to my face. Otherwise, I'll walk out that damn courtyard gate and hail a cab. You really think he's going to like that?"

V's eyebrows swoop together as he texts me again.

V: He's busy. On a call. You have to wait.

"At what point during the whole time you've known me have I made you think I'm cool with waiting? I will scream down this house, if that's what it takes. We don't need my dad calling the cops. You know that even better than I do."

V grunts again, and I shove my finger into his solid chest.

"Take me to him now, or we're going to have a serious problem that goes far beyond me being pissed as hell."

Another growl.

"Now." I jab harder, finding this whole giving-orders thing comes quite naturally to me.

V turns with a glare, jerking his head toward the door. I know enough about his body language to interpret it as *follow me.*

"See? Isn't it easier when you just do what I say?"

We head into the exterior hallway, and I follow behind him until we sneak into the rabbit warren of secret passageways through the painting entrance.

"Is there a map I'm going to get one of these days? Because I'd like to know how to get around myself."

V doesn't bother to answer, which is fine with me, because all I care about is getting to Lachlan as quickly as possible. Preferably before my dad has the entire police department combing the city for me and a black Maybach.

When the bookcase slides aside, V allows me to enter first but doesn't follow. Lachlan is seated at his desk and on his cell phone, arguing with someone. He stands as soon as he sees me.

His gaze clearly asks, *What are you doing?*

I respond quietly, practically mouthing the words. "I need to go to work before my dad calls the cops."

He holds up a finger and heads for the open doorway where V still stands. I pace, not feeling remotely patient as he continues speaking to whomever is on the other end of the call.

I block it out. I've already determined there are plenty of things I don't need to know about my husband's business.

When I reach the edge of his desk, I spin on my heel, preparing to pace in the opposite direction, but something on the monitor catches my eye.

I shriek as I step toward it, banging my hip on the corner of the desk. The shooting pain barely registers because the monitor shows a blond woman shackled to the hospital bed I recognize from the days after the car accident.

A blond woman. The woman who shot me and locked me in a mausoleum with a pile of dead bodies. Including my best friend's almost dead body.

"What the fuck?" I shout. "What the fucking fuck?"

Lachlan turns toward me. His expression goes blank as he lowers the phone and ends the call without a word. "Keira—"

He steps in my direction, but I hold out a hand at him as I point at the camera feed.

"You need to explain this right now. Right. Now. Because this doesn't make any sense."

"Keira—" He repeats my name, but it barely penetrates the buzzing in my ears.

"You said you took care of this. And when you said you took care of it, I *believed you*! You know why? Because every time you say that, it means you *fucking took care of it*!"

"Will you calm—"

"Don't you dare tell me to calm down! Is my husband

down there too? How many people do you have locked up in the basement?"

His expression, already hard, turns stony. "He's at the bottom of the fucking bayou, not in the goddamned basement."

I fling my hand wildly at the screen. "Then what the hell is she doing down there? She tried to kill me! She's the reason my best friend is in a coma! And what about the other women in that tomb? Why is she still alive?"

Lachlan's granite features dissolve into pure anguish. "Because I couldn't fucking kill her, okay? I couldn't fucking pull the trigger."

I grip the edge of the desk, my lungs heaving as I try to understand what the hell is going on here. Clearly, I'm missing something massive.

"Tell me why, Lachlan. You have to tell me why." I speak each word carefully, like my sanity depends on it, because it actually might.

My husband—who I'm beginning to question if I know *at all*—scrubs both hands over his face. "It's complicated."

"Then I suggest you uncomplicate it right now. I'm starting to wonder if I have a clue who you really are, and I really don't like wondering that."

With his fingers pressed to his temples, Lachlan's eyes close for a beat before fixing on me. "My past is ugly."

"And I married you knowing exactly what and who you are—at least, I thought I did." I point at the woman on the monitor. "She shot me. She told me she was your destiny. She said you were supposed to love *her*. I think I deserve an explanation."

Lachlan's face turns into that unreadable mask I've seen

too many times. "Then you better sit down, because this isn't a short story. It's the story of my fucking life."

I drop into his desk chair, my injuries protesting at the sudden movement, and I look at the image of the unconscious woman strapped to a hospital bed and then back at my husband.

"You can start whenever you're ready. Preferably now."

FIFTY-TWO

Mount

Thirteen years earlier

COLLEGE GRADUATION. THIS WAS THE FIRST ONE I'D ever attended, because I sure as hell didn't spend a day in college myself. Watching Destiny cross the stage and accept her diploma from MIT caused a rush of pride to roll through me.

After the ceremony, I waited outside among a crowd of families hugging and celebrating. I'd never felt more out of place in my life, regardless of how expensive my suit was.

When Destiny rushed through the crowd, she didn't stop to talk to anyone. Her eyes were locked on me, and she launched herself into my arms. Out of sheer instinct, I caught her.

"See? I did it!"

"Never doubted you for a second." Destiny had always been smart.

MEGHAN MARCH

"I wish . . . I wish Hope had been here to see it."

Guilt stabbed into me, sharper than the switchblade I carry in my pocket. I still didn't know whether I was responsible, or if she was dead before I got there. There was no way for me to ever put that guilt to rest.

I forced a smile onto my face when I looked at Destiny. "I'm sure she's looking down on you."

A smile trembled on her lips. "You think?"

"Of course."

"I think you're right."

Desperate to change the subject, I asked, "You ready?"

"Yeah. My apartment's packed."

I turned, but the words she just spoke stopped me before I could take a step. "I meant for dinner. Not to move. You're not coming back to New Orleans. There's nothing for you there."

Destiny, the girl I still remembered as the five-year-old whose door I slept outside of, crossed her arms with a stubborn tilt to her chin. "I'm coming back. I didn't bust my ass to learn all this stuff to put it to work for someone else."

"What the hell are you talking about?"

"I'm coming to work for you." Her tone was adamant, but not as adamant as mine.

"The fuck you are. Not a chance in hell. You wouldn't last a day in my world, Desi. You need to stay as far away from me and New Orleans as you can after today."

I headed for the car, her heels clicking on the sidewalk behind me as she hurried to catch up. I unlocked the rental as she stopped at the passenger side.

"Hand-to-hand combat. Sharpshooter training.

Microexpression identification. Tactical driving."

"What the fuck does that mean?"

"I've spent the last four years learning every single thing I could in and out of the classroom so I'd be an asset to the organization. An asset to *you*. You never wondered why I needed all that extra money for classes? This is why. If you think you're going to ship me off somewhere and expect me to stay away, then you don't know me very well."

"Destiny—"

"No. I'm J now. Isn't that how it works? First letter of my last name. You've spent almost twenty years protecting me, and now it's my turn. I will prove myself. I'm not a kid, Mount. I'm an asset. Use me."

"That's not why I sent you here. You've got a shot at a normal life—"

Destiny's expression twisted into one of mock humor. "Really? Because I don't come from the same shit that you do? You think somehow I'm going to turn into Suzy Homemaker and pop out a few kids for some upper-middle-class salesman who probably fucks his secretary? Is that what you really want for me?"

"I'd kill him."

Her smile turned triumphant. "Exactly. And if anyone crosses you, I'll kill them. It's my turn to repay what you've done for me my whole life. I'll prove to you that I'm strong enough. That I'm good enough. This is how it's always been meant to be, Mount. You and me against the world."

I yanked open the door and took a seat inside, jamming the key into the ignition as she settled into the passenger seat. As I started the car, I wished I could say I didn't understand where she was coming from with this, but I did. I knew what it was like to want to prove your worth. To prove that you belonged somewhere.

"Don't make me regret this, J." I shot her a sharp look as I shifted into reverse.

"I've got your back, boss. You'll see."

FIFTY-THREE

Keira

Present day

WITH EACH STORY HE TELLS ME ABOUT HOPE AND Destiny and what they endured, especially the part about carrying Hope's body out of the burning house while Destiny watched, my heart shatters into smaller and smaller pieces.

Not for myself, but for them. All of them. For the children they never got to be. For the chance they never got at a normal life.

Lachlan has spent the last hour telling me everything. Well, telling my shoulder. Or the wall. Or the ceiling.

Until he finally meets my gaze, and the pain and anguish in his is almost more than I can bear.

"If she were anyone else, she'd already be dead for what she did to you. But I couldn't pull the trigger. It makes me the biggest fucking hypocrite in the world, because I wiped a goddamned cartel out of this city for spilling your blood, and she was the one who put it all in motion. She hired a low-level cartel member to take the shot. They didn't order it, she did, and I've spent the last week while you were in the hospital undoing the damage she caused. She's the reason I cut a deal with the other cartel. They're taking responsibility, and in exchange, they get a monopoly on sourcing all the drug trade in the city." He glances up at the ceiling again. "And still, I couldn't put a bullet in her brain like she deserves. Fuck, I couldn't even order someone else to do it, because I'm—"

I cut him off. "Not the monster you thought you were? Because you're human?"

Lachlan's hard gaze cuts to mine. "No—"

I stand and walk around the desk, coming toward the man I married, realizing that in some ways, I know him better than he knows himself.

"You shouldn't—"

"Love you? Tell you that after everything you've shared with me, I couldn't kill her either if I were you? Because that's exactly what I'm telling you."

Carefully, I lower myself onto his lap and pull his stiff arm around me.

He watches me with confusion creasing his brow. "You should want her dead for what she did to you and Magnolia. And, God . . . the rest of them."

My stomach twists at the thought of all those bodies in that mausoleum, but I shove it down. "How can I want her dead when you've been watching out for her practically her whole life? She's like a little sister to you. None of you got a fair chance, not from the beginning. She's broken, Lachlan. You didn't do that. Her life did."

"That doesn't mean she's not culpable for her actions." His words sound almost as rusty as V's did.

"She's as culpable as anyone who's criminally insane. Her mind isn't right. You can't tell me it is."

He looks away, his jaw tense. "She's a fucking genius, Keira. She graduated at the top of her class at MIT. I won't make excuses for her—"

I grip his chin and turn his face back to me. "Then I will. Because she can be a genius all day long and still have severe mental-health issues that she's done an incredible job of hiding from you. She needs *help*."

He swallows, his Adam's apple bobbing. "And how the hell do I help her? She knows too much for me to hand her off to some clinic to put on lockdown somewhere."

"You're richer than God, Lachlan. Don't tell me you can't get her help and keep your secrets safe at the same time."

He lowers his head until his forehead rests against mine. "This has been tearing me apart since the second I realized what she'd done."

"Then let me help put you back together. We're a team. There's nothing we can't handle."

He lifts his head, and something akin to awe softens his features. "I don't deserve you."

"Good thing I know you're wrong. Now, come on, you have shit to figure out. Plans to put into motion, because that's what you do. And I have to go to work before my dad calls the fucking FBI."

Lachlan buries his hand in my hair and whispers two words. "*Thank you.*"

FIFTY-FOUR

Keira

Three months later

"**W**HERE THE HELL ARE WE GOING?" LACHLAN growls the question in my ear as we climb the stairs to his jet. The jet I requested be fueled and ready for the honeymoon I planned.

I turn around and shoot him a saucy smile. "Remember that time you didn't tell me we were going to Dublin until we were already in the air? Consider this turnabout being fair play. Besides, growl all you want. I think it's sexy."

"Keira—"

"Patience, husband. Patience."

His gaze skewers me, but he doesn't say anything else. I'm pretty sure it takes everything he has not to march to the cockpit and demand our destination from the pilot. The pilot I've sworn to secrecy with the threat of losing his job.

It turns out, when I issue threats now, people take them seriously.

That doesn't mean the last two months haven't been without their challenges, however. Destiny is settled into a locked-down facility where she receives round-the-clock care and a boatload of counseling and medication. She's officially been diagnosed with dissociative identity disorder. She's also smart as hell, and has tried to escape multiple times. Thankfully, the massive amount of security on the premises has foiled every attempt before she got too far. She's done a lot of talking, though, including about how she's known for years that Hope was buried in that mausoleum, because she'd followed Lachlan on the anniversary of her sister's death and watched him lay flowers at the doors.

Magnolia finally woke up, praise the Lord, but doesn't remember anything about what happened. I think it's better that way. She's on "leave" from her job, because she's also undergoing a lot of physical and occupational therapy. She definitely is receiving sister-of-the-queen benefits.

The distillery is chugging along, making the best whiskey in the country. Then again, I'm biased. Even though the rackhouse caught fire, all was not lost. Smoke and flames damaged several of the barrels, but my father, with a lifetime of experience, had a hypothesis that was genius—the smoke and char on the barrels added a totally different flavor to the whiskey, in a good way. When we bottled a few of the barrels that were properly aged, the flavor was incredible. Something we might never be able to duplicate, and due to the scarcity, the price has skyrocketed.

Seven Sinners' Phoenix Label is now one of the rarest and most expensive whiskeys on the market. We're experimenting with smoking and charring our barrels, but this time, without the fire department needing to be called in.

We also launched the Spirit of New Orleans on a limited release, and the response has been phenomenal. Our expansion project has been moved to the top of the priority list because we need more capacity *yesterday*. As soon as the expansion project is complete in about sixty days, we'll start tours of the facility, and New Orleans will have a brand-new attraction.

Mom and Dad went back to Florida after about a month, but before they left, my dad told me something I've been waiting years to hear.

"I wouldn't have been able to leave this company in anyone else's hands. You've done me proud, Keira, and you've done things I never dreamed Seven Sinners could accomplish. Your grandfather and his father before him would be proud too. You're a credit to the family name, my girl."

I still haven't told my parents I don't actually bear the family name anymore, or that the rock on my hand isn't just an engagement ring. When I asked my husband for advice, his response was simple. *"Tell them or don't. Whenever and whatever you want. I'll always make sure they're safe regardless."*

Yeah . . . I'm still working on that, although I'm pretty sure my dad figured it out. He's not dumb, and V's constant presence around the distillery is a dead giveaway that something is very, very different.

But shockingly, Dad didn't push, and somehow, he kept my mom from asking questions too.

I don't live in the light anymore, but Lachlan doesn't live solely in the shadows either. We've found a happy medium, and that happy medium is heading out of the country so we can be Lachlan and Keira again like we were in Dublin.

When I attempt to take the seat next to him, he pulls me onto his lap.

"You're going to tell me. I demand to know."

"You *demand*? That's pretty serious. I mean, what with your reputation and all."

"Damn right, hellion. You should fear me, because I own you."

Even though his tone is dark and gritty, I can't help but smile.

"You own me . . . hmm? So, does that mean my ass is yours? Or did I wear this monster butt plug for no reason?"

Shock. It's not an expression I see often on his face, but it's definitely there now.

"Excuse me?"

I force my expression into mock severity. "I don't repeat myself."

His dark gaze flares with heat. "Then I guess I'm going to have to find out for myself if what I thought I heard was right."

The jet hurtles down the runway as his lips crash into mine. I squirm on his lap as the heat that was already present between my legs ratchets up about a hundred degrees.

By the time we reach cruising altitude, I'm missing my shirt, and we're tangled up on the long sofa in the back of the plane.

"You need a jet with a bedroom. Time to upgrade, Lachlan."

"If I'd known I'd fall in love with a woman who pushed me to the edge just by breathing, I would've gotten one."

I still as the words leave his lips. "You love me?"

It's been months, and even though I was pretty certain

Lachlan Mount loved me—because if nothing else, he's a man of action rather than words—I've still wanted to hear the words.

"Are you fucking crazy, hellion? Of course I love you. The thought of losing you almost killed me. I've never known how to love anyone, but you taught me. You made it impossible *not* to love you."

I bite my lip as tears burn behind my eyes.

"Don't you dare cry. Not now."

"Don't tell me what to do, Lachlan Mount."

"I'll tell you what to do anytime I want, Keira Mount. Especially when you're naked."

The burn of the tears dissipates. "Don't threaten me with a good time."

His lips descend onto mine, taking over, just like he always does. "Tell me where we're going," he demands against my mouth.

"No. Not yet."

"How long do you think you'll be able to hold out while I keep you on the edge of orgasm?"

"I guess we'll see."

FIFTY-FIVE

Mount

"**P**LEASE! JUST LET ME COME!"

"Tell me."

My wife bares her teeth at me like a wild animal. I can attest to the fact that she is by the scratches on my back, and I wouldn't have her any other way.

I press against the plug in her ass, loving how her wetness drips down to it as I tease her piercing with my tongue.

"No!"

"Stubborn, stubborn hellion." I toy with the plug. "I bet when I sink my cock into this tight little ass, you'll scream my name and whatever else I want to know."

She arches her back, lifting toward me.

In all reality, I couldn't care less where we're going, but being with Keira—especially locked in a battle of wills that's playing out naked—is my most favorite thing in the world.

"Try me." She grits out the words, desperately reaching to steal her orgasm, and I let her have it because I can't deny her anything for long.

When she screams my name, I'm actually proud she held out against telling me. I've never liked surprises before, but with Keira, everything is different.

Life isn't black and white anymore. It's filled with color, and not just gold.

"Are you going to follow through, Lachlan, or did I do all this prep work for nothing?"

She challenges me every day. It keeps me on my toes—and my dick hard—nearly 24/7.

"Oh, hellion, you should know better than to test me."

I pull the plug from her ass and grab the lube she had stashed in her purse. Have I mentioned she's also the most resourceful woman I've ever met?

I coat my fingers before I pull the plug free, filling her nearly virgin hole with a finger. "Who owns this ass?"

Her expression turns mulish. "I do."

I push a second finger inside and press a button on the remote beside me. "Want to try again?"

"That is so not fair!" Her voice rises an octave as she presses into my touch, vibrations ripping through her body from the toy in her pussy. "I'm going to come."

"Not until I'm buried deep inside that ass I own. My woman. My wife. My *love*."

A tender expression flashes across her face. "You don't play fair."

"I never have. I never will. Not when it comes to you. Now, tell me what I want to hear." I move my fingers in and out, and her muscles clench.

"I love you."

"And?"

FIFTY-SIX

Keira

I SWEAR, HE ALWAYS WINS.

But lucky for me, when he wins, *I win*.

Lachlan pulls his fingers free and grabs a wet wipe I stashed with the lube. Because while I might still technically be a virgin in this area, I've got plenty of experience now. He coats his cock with the lube, and I tense as he presses the head against my tightest hole.

With a tug, he pulls the remote-operated vibrator out of my pussy and presses it against my piercing.

"That isn't fair!"

He pushes himself forward just enough to breach the ring of muscle, making my nerve endings zing with pleasure and sparks burst across my vision.

"Tell me," he says as he teases my clit.

"I belong to you." Triumph flares in his gaze as he pushes inside, and the sensations have me moaning the last part of my declaration. "But you belong to *me*."

As he buries his cock in my ass, my husband smiles.

"You better fucking believe it. Body. Heart. Soul."

He pulls back and fucks into me, but I'm already on the edge of orgasm.

I come again and again until he roars his climax and it echoes in the cabin of the plane. Our hearts hammer in time, sweat dripping from both our brows.

"Now, where the hell are we going?"

I smile. "You'll see."

FIFTY-SEVEN

Mount

As the plane touches down on the runway, Keira pulls a folder from her bag and hands it to me.

"What is this?"

"Don't get mad . . ."

I tense at the caution pervading her tone. "Why would I get mad?"

"Because I stole your DNA, submitted it under a false name using a PO box . . ."

I blink twice, replaying her statement in my head. "Why the hell would you do that?"

I snatch the folder from her hand and stare down at it. I've never wanted to know about the woman who left me in front of a church, but I can't deny I've always wondered about my roots, especially after seeing how Keira felt when she saw Dublin.

"Because I wanted you to know where you come from. I wanted to be able to tell our kids what their heritage is— from both sides of the family."

My gaze cuts to her face. "Are you—"

Keira shakes her head. "Not yet. But I definitely want to talk about it soon."

Kids. A family. Things I never considered before her, but think about all the time now. I used to avoid any connection for fear of weakness, but now I have no doubt that she's my greatest strength. She gives me a reason to wake up every morning and rule our empire with honor. Even if it's tarnished and dented.

I open the folder, and the results are on the first page.

73% Italy/Greece

"So, where the hell are we?" I lift my eyes from the page, shocked beyond belief.

"Greece. I thought we'd start here and see what you think. Sicily is next. Seemed appropriate. Then I figured we could head wherever you want to go next from there."

"I don't know what to say."

"You don't have to say anything. I just wanted to give you something I didn't think you'd ever give yourself. Something you gave me—a chance to see where I came from."

"I'm . . . literally fucking speechless."

"And that's totally fine. But in case you're wondering, it doesn't matter where you came from. All that matters is that you became the man you are. The one I love. The one I'm going to spend the rest of my life with. The one I'm going to raise a family with. And someday, the man who's going to meet my parents, preferably before we have our first kid."

She says the last part on a laugh, and I stand and pull her from her seat.

"They can meet us in Italy. Greece is our honeymoon. No parents allowed."

A smile breaks over Keira's face.

"Deal."

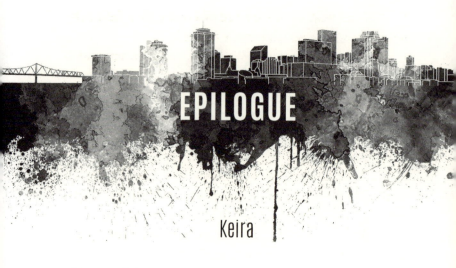

EPILOGUE

Keira

One month later – Mardi Gras

SOMETIMES, MAKING A DEAL WITH THE DEVIL IS THE best thing you can ever do. Especially when you realize he's not the devil at all.

Except tonight.

I school my features into a smile at the toy vibrating inside me as I listen to the owner of the New Orleans Voodoo Kings extoll the virtues of Seven Sinners whiskey, and his new favorite—the Phoenix Label.

"I'm so glad you're enjoying it."

"I'll be buying up as much as I can. I bet the commissioner would enjoy a bottle or two. And here I thought you couldn't top the Spirit of New Orleans."

"I'll make sure to hold a few bottles back for you, sir."

"I'd appreciate it," he says before taking another sip.

"If you'll excuse me for just a moment, I need to check on a few things."

"Of course. Y'all throw a hell of a party. We'll definitely be bringing the boys back in the future."

By *the boys*, he means the entire football team, and I barely hold myself back from fist pumping. "We'll look forward to making future arrangements with you soon."

"Thank you, Ms. Kilgore."

I step away from him and tense as vibrations rip through my body.

Lachlan and I nearly went to war over the fact that he wanted to completely take over security for the event. I disagreed, because Seven Sinners is *my* baby.

"Considering the fact that I'd like you to be having my *baby, I have a right to keep you safe."*

"You better not start this now. I'm not even pregnant."

"I'll start whenever I want. You're my wife."

Our argument escalated to bellowing in our suite, and ended with us tearing off each other's clothes in a frenzy, which is pretty much how all our arguments end.

In the aftermath, with the sheets tangled around us, Lachlan proposed a compromise. My security would be supplemented as necessary by his, but he wouldn't take control.

I agreed.

But when I stepped into the living room tonight in my ball gown, he was waiting in his perfectly tailored suit, holding a familiar-looking leather box. When he flipped the lid open, a black-and-gold toy lay inside, looking innocent, even though I knew it was far from it.

"You can put it in, or I will. But you're not leaving without it."

"This is a business event, Lachlan."

"*Tick tock*, Keira." He looked down at his watch. "You have fifteen minutes before we're supposed to leave."

I growled, a habit I picked up from him, and countered. "Only if you get on your knees first." I lifted one stiletto-clad foot to the chair and pulled up the full skirt of my gown so he could see the sparkling thong beneath it.

His dark gaze flashed. "Only for you. *Gladly* for you."

"Damn right."

Fast-forward three hours, and I'm dying for him to drag me off into a corner so I can beg him to fuck me—but first I have to find him in this sea of giants wearing Mardi Gras masks to match their flashy tailored suits.

I nod and smile, thankful that my face is obscured so no one sees my *almost O* face, and spend the next half hour looking for him as he torments me relentlessly.

Where the hell did he go? I'm going to kill him when I find him.

V is stationed near the elevator, wearing a mask. He asked for this post so he could keep an eye on the kitchen and Odile. I'm not sure what's happening there, but he's become protective of her. Mostly, I'm just happy to see that he's capable of smiling, especially since I've never heard him speak again.

"Where the hell is my husband?" I whisper in his ear.

He points down.

"My office?"

V nods.

That tricky son of a bitch.

I take the elevator down, but it stops on the first floor before I hit the basement.

At the front desk, Temperance is arguing with a tall, built man in a suit, explaining our no-return-of-keys policy.

"You got this?" I call to her, holding the elevator doors open.

She turns to look at me as the man glares down at her. "Of course, boss. He plays games for a living. Definitely nothing I can't handle."

The man's nostrils flare, and I consider stepping out of the elevator to defuse the situation, but the toy inside me buzzes to life again. I grip the metal bar on the elevator wall to stay upright.

I remind myself that Z is outside as well. *She'll be fine*, I tell myself. *What's the worst that could happen?*

I hit the DOOR CLOSE button and tap my foot in anticipation as they slide shut and the elevator descends to the basement.

As I approach my office, I hear footsteps coming from inside, and I'm brought back to the second night Lachlan Mount changed my life. I yank my door open and peer inside at the dim light pooling on my desk.

"What do you want?" I whisper. "Why are you here?"

He rises to his feet, those wide fingers refastening the button on his suit, his face hidden in the shadows.

"You owe me a debt, Mrs. Mount, and I'm here to collect."

The End

243

Go to www.meghanmarch.com/#!newsletter/c1uhp
to sign up for my newsletter, and never miss another
announcement about upcoming projects, new releases,
sales, exclusive excerpts, and giveaways.

ALSO BY MEGHAN MARCH

Take Me Back

Bad Judgment

BENEATH SERIES:
Beneath These Shadows
Beneath This Mask
Beneath This Ink
Beneath These Chains
Beneath These Scars
Beneath These Lies
Beneath the Truth

DIRTY BILLIONAIRE TRILOGY:
Dirty Billionaire
Dirty Pleasures
Dirty Together

ACKNOWLEDGMENTS

I knew Mount and Keira's story was special when Mount stormed into my brain in October 2016 and took up residence. He was demanding. Commanding. Consuming. When it was finally his turn, he flipped my world on its head by unleashing an even more epic story than I knew was coming. I knew within three days of drafting that there was no way this could be contained in one book. I poured my heart and soul and every raw emotion into this project, and it almost broke me. One thing is for certain—I couldn't have done this alone. Every book takes a village, but this story took an army.

Although I usually save him for last, I have to thank my incredible man for holding all the pieces of me together when I was falling apart due to lack of sleep, deadline stress, and the twists and turns of the most intense plot I've ever conquered. He's my biggest cheerleader and greatest strength. Thank you, JDW, for all that you do. I love you so much.

Angela Smith – Wow. We rocked what seemed like the impossible task. Thank you for being there every step of the way as I worked my way through this story. You are truly an amazing woman, and I am so grateful to have you on my team and as a cherished friend.

My JJL Crew – You gave me the pep talks to end all pep

talks, especially Mo, to get my ass in gear and finish this book when I thought it would break me. We can never, ever break up. Love you all.

Pam Berehulke – As always, you are the calm in the tempestuous storm of my ever-changing schedule. Please, please, never stop doing what you do. I absolutely love working with you on every project we tackle. Thank you so much for your attention to detail and flawless professionalism.

Danielle Sanchez – Even when my creative muse decides to disrupt all of our best-laid plans, you adapt and change as quickly as I do. Thank you for your support and ideas and encouragement.

Jamie Lynn – I can't thank you enough for keeping me sane and holding down the fort when I disappear into the dark depths of the writing cave. I am so lucky to have you on my team, and I can't wait to see where we go next!

Kim and Natasha – Thank you for being extraordinary beta readers and helping me make sure Mount and Keira's story was everything I hoped it could be. Your time is a gift, and I appreciate it more than you know.

Julie Deaton and Michelle Lim – You are my rock-star proofreaders! Thank you for your eagle eyes and fabulously fast turnaround!

Letitia Hassar – When one cover morphed into three, you

rocked amazing designs. Thank you for your creativity and skills!

Sara Eirew – Thank you for capturing the perfect images for this trilogy!

AUTHOR'S NOTE

UNAPOLOGETICALLY SEXY ROMANCE

I'd love to hear from you. Connect with me at:

Website: www.meghanmarch.com
Facebook: www.facebook.com/MeghanMarchAuthor
Twitter: www.twitter.com/meghan_march
Instagram: www.instagram.com/meghanmarch

ABOUT THE AUTHOR

Meghan March has been known to wear camo face paint and tromp around in the woods wearing mud-covered boots, all while sporting a perfect manicure. She's also impulsive, easily entertained, and absolutely unapologetic about the fact that she loves to read and write smut.

Her past lives include slinging auto parts, selling lingerie, making custom jewelry, and practicing corporate law. Writing books about dirty-talking alpha males and the strong, sassy women who bring them to their knees is by far the most fabulous job she's ever had.

She loves hearing from her readers at meghanmarch-books@gmail.com.

90044978R00155

Made in the USA
Columbia, SC
25 February 2018